HEART OF LIES

CONNOR WHITELEY

ACKNOWLEDGMENTS

Thank you to all my readers, without you I couldn't do what I love.

CHAPTER 1

Stretching out her hands, Alessandria lightly touched the hard cold dark brown oak arms of her throne as she sat down.

She adjusted herself in her seat. Feeling the soft black pillows moulding to her flesh. Sending cold chills through her body as the material warmed up after the freezing weather last night.

Turning her head, Alessandria rolled her eyes at the boring yet imposing cold grey stone blocks of pure might that made up the small chamber she sat in. The blocks of stone gave a chill to the air and a reminder that they were deep in the Queen's castle that no one could hear you scream.

Of course, Alessandria hadn't tested that fact yet but she wanted to at some point.

Stretching her neck, Alessandria gave a small smile at the curved ceiling with all the blades tied to it. She had no idea why someone tied or welded the blades to the ceiling but they were always helpful reminders to the criminals she dealt with.

That reminded her, she needed to get some new scented candles since the candles burned in the four corners stunk of animal fat and sweat. Not pleasant. And certainly not what a noble woman was used to!

Yet as always Alessandria focused on her purpose, sure everything wasn't as she planned when she had accepted the Queen's offer to live in the castle. But at least her noble family had a home and somewhere to base their operations.

Alessandria turned her head to the left and peeked out a small glass window that bright sunlight poured in from. Squeaking her eyes, she saw the massive clock tower outside and rolled her eyes.

They were ten minutes late. Alessandria didn't mind personally hearing cases from her Procurators when they weren't sure what the law said. But the least the Procurators could do was be on time. It wasn't like Alessandria was a busy Noble woman or anything. At least, it was only 10 past 8 in the morning. Hopefully, at least she could do something later if the meeting overran.

Casting her mind back to her first case hearing, she hated it. It was an hour after she was promoted to Dominus Procurator and she had to decide whether to forward a murder case to the Crown Prosecution Service. It was difficult because the victim was horrible but it was still murder. She decided against it because the victim was a horrible scammer and deserved it.

Hopefully, this occasion would be less of a difficult choice.

A loud scraping sound filled the chamber as the immense heavy wooden door opened and three people walked in.

The first Alessandria easily recognised as one of her Procurators, Police Officers, she looked like your typical Procurator with her grey cloak and her black leather armour underneath. Yet her violet eyes and long black hair made her easy to recognise.

Whilst not Alessandria's favourite Procurator, since this one was pretty average, she could tolerate this Procurator for a while.

The other two women Alessandria supposed were the people she was judging. She raised an eyebrow at both of them with their dirty slimy brown dresses and their greasy hair.

At least the women to Alessandria's right had the decency to wear some horrific perfume that stunk of… Alessandria had no idea, but it stunk.

The Procurator started in her very common and unprofessional tone: "Ya Lady, this are the two I spoke of,"

"What is the situation?" Alessandria elegantly spoke looking at the women.

The Procurator was about to speak but Alessandria raised a hand.

"Um, Miss, um my Lady," the lady to her right greeted.

"Speak," Alessandria ordered.

"That woman stole 50 coins from me and a week's food!" the other woman shouted.

Alessandria looked at the accused with her narrowing eyes.

"Theft is a serious offence in my land. Do not think because my family is not based on our land. It does not mean will let our land go lawless,"

"Um, Miss, I swear I didn't steal it,"

"Liar!"

Alessandria raised a hand to silence the accuser.

"What do you believed happened Procurator?"

"Ya Lady, the woman definitely stole food and money. It's a shame,"

"Why bring this to me if you are sure? I am the Dominicus Procurator. I have more cases to investigate and oversee. I hope you are not wasting my time,"

"Na Lady, this woman. The theft I thought you might want to hear her side,"

"Fine, tell me your side,"

"Um, Miss, I didn't steal it. I was going to give it back,"

"Liar!"

"Be silent or I will grab one of these weapons on the ceiling and kill you with it!" Alessandria shouted as she smiled.

The woman went silent.

Alessandria smiled as she made a note to remember that for the future.

"Um, I was going to give it back. I need the coin for my son. He needs to go to school,"

"Education is free, you know that,"

"Um, miss, but my son is bright. Too bright for the normal schools they said. They won't take him. He wants to become a doctor one day. I cannot afford the education he needs,"

"How old is your son?"

"Ten, Miss,"

Alessandria understood the mother's concern. All the doctors in the land were from the noble families or the richest families. A mere common woman would never be able to get their child educated enough to even be considered by the Medicus Colleges. But stealing?

"What about the food?"

"Um, Miss. I work two jobs. I see my son for two hours a day. My mother looks after him. She cannot work. I sleep for four hours a night. I can barely feed us,"

"And what about me and my family!"

Alessandria nodded. Despite all the financial support her family gave to her people. It was never enough. Too many people in need and not enough money.

However, she had everything she needed to know. Yet this was difficult if she found the thief guilty then the bright child would lose another parent. He might never become a doctor and get his family out of poverty.

If she didn't find her guilty then people would question her and she would be called weak and unfit by others. Then what sort of precedence does that set for all other poor people that want to steal?

"I have made my decision," Alessandria turned to face the thief. "I hereby decree you are found guilty, but I will not charge you. You are to give back the coin and the food,"

The other woman nodded with thanks.

The thief fell to her knees with tears swelling up in her eyes.

"And I will write to the Head of the School Board and get your son a place at a good school. My family will pay for it. Providing you do not commit more crimes and your son becomes a doctor in the future for the people of my land,"

"Um, Miss. Of course, of course. Thank you!"

"Dismissed," Alessandria waved them away.

All three women bowed and ran away.

Alessandria stretched her arms and felt the warm wood of the wooden throne as she heard heavy footsteps walking towards her.

As soon as she saw the blue and fiery armour, she knew it was Nemesio. Her complex memories returned to her mind as she remembered how the former Inquisitor got her brother kidnapped and tortured and tried to destroy her family. Yet he was trying to make amends, so she was putting up with him.

Although, she hated to admit looking at him in his tight armour was semi-pleasing. She shook the thoughts away as he stopped in front of her.

"Impressive judgement. Both people got what they wanted,"

"I try and that woman did the wrong thing for the right reasons,"

Nemesio smiled and nodded.

"Are you ready?" Nemesio asked.

Alessandria paused before saying: "Of course, we have this Queen thing again,"

"Yes. We are meant to be protecting the Queen,"

Alessandria stood up from her throne and they both started to walk towards the door.

"I know. I know. It's been three weeks since she's hired us and we still don't know who's trying to kill her,"

"One of my contacts said something might change today,"

"Well, Nemesio. Time to save a Queen,"

CHAPTER 2

Placing my large cream mug filled with almost black bitter coffee down on the desk, I signed another military contract and added it to the ever growing pile.

I do love having a clear desk as I admired the smooth oak wood of the desk with its lumps and bumps and the gold running in between random splits in the wood. Even the wooden draws and legs were covered in gold.

Of course, this was overkill but I wasn't going to deny the Queen when she gave me an office in the heart of the castle. Although, I have to admit the cold stone walls with no other furniture was boring. Perhaps I'll grab Harrison later and go shopping with him for some cabinets and decorations.

Personally, I don't see the big deal about having a big perfect homely office but my assistant was moaning earlier. I suppose that's one of the reasons why I prefer autistic people. None of us care about these little things as much.

Shaking my head at the thought of going shopping with all those people and the noise, I spun my dulled blade in my left hand and took another slip of my coffee. Letting my tongue enjoy the bitter chocolatey notes of the coffee.

Placing the mug back down, I breathed in coffee scents that filled the office and I made a note to thank Harrison for buying me this coffee. He said earlier that it was expensive since it came from far away. I told him that wasn't logical but he agreed and said that's what boyfriends are meant to do for one another. Not sure if I agree but I appreciated the gesture.

Returning to the task at hand, I looked at the last military contract on my desk and I opened it. Feeling the cold paper and its rough edges.

Although, as I read it, I got more and more confused. It was something about the Head of the Military requesting over a thousand men, two thousand swords and enough rations to last them a year.

My eyebrows rose. As the person who dealt with all the contracts for the family business I know this wasn't abnormal for the Military to order such large quantities from us. Since we control the Military trade in the country but I didn't understand why he would only pay a thousand coins to us. Especially, when all this would cost four times that to produce, not including the rations.

I reread the contract and it said nothing about the reasons for the request and the Queen hadn't signed the contract to give her blessing. So, I smiled and I thankfully rejected it.

However, the oddity of the request troubled me. I remember Alessandria mentioning something about her and that awful Nemesio being tasked with finding the people who want the Queen dead. Could they be connected?

Picking up my coffee once more to finish it, I guess I'll mention it to my sister when I see her. But I am not talking to that Nemesio not after what he did. Even at the thought of the former Inquisitor I spun my dulled blade rapidly.

"You okay beautiful?"

I raised my head with a boyish smile as I looked at Harrison in his stunning expensive black suit that highlighted his slight muscles, and slim frame.

I stood up, walked over to him, and gave him a quick hug and kiss. Breathing in his beautiful earthy aftershave.

"I'm better now. But you aren't actually dragging me along to this royalty thing, are you?"

Harrison gave a small laugh.

"Daniel, you are coming. And all the important people will be there,"

"But the noise, the crowd. I don't like noise and crowds. Too many people,"

My dulled blade spun even faster.

"Beautiful, I hate noise as much as you do. I hate people more than you, but I'm Head of the Queen's Engineers. I have duties,"

"As do I,"

"Your desk is clear,"

Sometimes my autistic productivity is a curse!

I suppose I could go to this event. After all I get to see Alessandria and talk to her. But will I be able to cope with all those people?

Clearly, my face must have been conflicted as Harrison wrapped his strong arms around me.

"Daniel, we will be fine. You have your dulled blade to play with and I have my tricks. And please, just do it for me,"

Who could resist such a nice plea?

"Fine. You own me though,"

"I know how to make it up to you,"

I backed away as I pushed his arms away. I knew what he meant but... I wasn't sure. Normal people could easily do it by three weeks of dating. I wasn't sure on my opinion. Could I deal with being touched for that long?

Harrison stepped over to me.

I got a whiff of his earthy aftershave.

"Daniel, I'm sorry. I know you want to and that's enough. I can wait,"

I gave him a slow nod.

Well, he had a point. This was my dream to do it, but I don't know if I can handle the touching for so long. As much as I love my autism, this is probably the one area I'm concerned or conflicted about.

Looking around, I picked up the file. This was strange and something wasn't right. The Queen always signs the contracts to make it a legal request, so why was this contract so different? Especially, with the amounts of military might requested. Something was wrong and hopefully I would find something at this forsaken event.

So, I grabbed Harrison's hand and we left.

CHAPTER 3

After all the boring formalities of shaking the hands and greeting all the important people of Ordericous, Alessandria, Nemesio and Hellen had finally made it to the stage along with lots of other people. Making the air hot and humid and the chamber smelled... interesting as Alessandria breathed in all the different sweet, fruity and earthy perfumes everyone wore.

Alessandria had never minded greeting the Nobility whenever her family had guests but she didn't need to greet all the military captains and commanders, the Nobility and everyone of importance in the castle and church. She probably shook over a hundred hands.

Yet it didn't matter now as Alessandria stood on the far right hand edge of the large wooden stage next to Hellen and Nemesio.

Scanning the chamber, Alessandria eyed all the members of the crowd. She eyed the military leaders at the back, all the church people who snarled at Daniel to the left and all the rich families to the right. All chatting and muttering to themselves.

Alessandria hoped Daniel was okay with all this noise.

Alessandria's eyes narrowed on them all, she wanted to see if someone was an assassin before they striked, but who knew an assassin would attack?

Turning her head slightly, Alessandria looked at the six massive guards in thick imposing armour with red metal shields as tall as her, standing behind and in front of the Queen. Then Alessandria smiled briefly as she caught Daniel's eye as he looked at her.

Daniel smiled and looked away. Continuing to spin his dulled blade fast.

She wished Daniel would come over and be with her. They were siblings but she couldn't blame him for avoiding her when Nemesio was around. It probably explained why Daniel had placed Harrison in between Nemesio and himself. Whilst she was determined to prove to Daniel that Nemesio was sorry for getting him tortured, she knew she just needed to support and love him.

Raising her head, Alessandria focused on the rows of burning candles in the ceiling and the great sheets of stain glass that illuminated the chamber. Even one would have been a perfect place for an assassin to lie in wait. Yet that was assuming there was an assassin.

Despite Nemesio's faith in his informant, Alessandria knew better than to have complete faith in them. As she remembered some interesting situations of informants lying and the traps she had walked into during her Procurator days.

After a few moments, the Queen in her admittedly stunning white armour started her speech as she stood in the centre of the stage.

"My dearest subjects and friends, I have bought you here today to celebrate the ending of the war against Mortisical,"

Hellen and I smiled as we heard the military moaning and muttering to themselves. She tapped my feet with her big wooden stick as I almost laughed aloud.

"I know this may have come as a shock. We were winning the war against the people of Mortisical, but the war should never have happened in the first place,"

Hellen gave a few silent laughs as a wave of moaning came from the military lot at the back.

"My military commanders, I will not be disrespected. One more sound from you and I shall remove you all from your current positions,"

That silenced them quickly.

Afterwards, the Queen continued to explain why she ended the war and the secret peace treaty that she negotiated with her foreign counterparts.

Alessandria continued to smile in support of her Queen as she spoke, but Alessandria understood the military's outrage. A lot of good men including her father had died during this war. And all of her family, except her mother, had fought in the war.

Although, Alessandria doubted her father would have cared. He never really understood the war and neither did she. The former King said it was something about a transgression and a terror attack. Yet nobody really bought it, so she supposed it was only right his daughter stopped a war built on lies.

A part of her considered her family because war was their business, but she thought about the money her family makes off the training of the soldiers alone. At least, she didn't need to worry about getting a job for a long time.

Turning her attention to the crowd, Alessandria started to notice people walking very slowly towards the stage.

In the crowd of hundreds, it might have been only twenty people. Not a lot but just enough for her to notice the crowd moving.

Hellen tapped her legs. Alessandria nodded.

She looked at the Queen, who was metres away. Too far to run to protect her.

A piece of her mind considered this wasn't a group of killers, but she knew better.

Narrowing her eyes, Alessandria focused on the moving crowd. They were too far away.

She looked in Daniel's direction and he too was looking at something. Alessandria didn't know what, but her brother was observant. He probably saw them before she did.

Then the people in the crowd stopped moving.

Alessandria's heart raced.

Nothing happened.

Alessandria turned her attention to the Queen.

"And as I decreed in the Peace treaty, in exchange for friendships and trade, I am hereby decreeing all our forces to return here immediately. All operations are to stop in Mortisical!"

The military commanders shouted, and the Church people screamed about the missionaries they had lost.

The crowd moved in a wave of anger.

Alessandria tensed.

People moved through the crowd.

Alessandria needed to see a weapon.

She couldn't scream out a warning without proof.

The Queen's guards slammed their shields down.

The crowd got angrier.

Nemesio tensed.

Someone in a black cloak was approaching the stage.

They paced towards the Queen.

Alessandria saw a pistol.

"Assassin!" she screamed. Running at the Queen.

The guards instantly formed a wall around the Queen.

The assassin fired.

A shot screamed through the air.

Hitting a Guard's shield.

People screamed.

They ran.

Alessandria jumped off the stage.

She looked around.

The assassin was gone.

"For the Triad!" people screamed as twenty people in dark cloaks charged towards the stage.

CHAPTER 4

At least with the Queen speaking it stopped all those awful noises of the pointless people muttering and chatting. I do hate noise even a whisper can sometimes sound like a shout.

Looking around the immense stone chamber with the rows of burning candles and sunlight coming through the ugly stained glass windows. I acknowledged the fools in the crowd. From the pompous and ultimately useless military commanders and captains to the hateful Church people that stunk of so-called smelly holy oil. Even now they sneered at me and Harrison.

In all honesty, I had kissed Harrison rather publicly earlier just to annoy them. Sure it was petty but I didn't care. Being Nobility does have advantages.

However, as the Queen revealed the end of the war and loud noises started again. I spun my dulled blade quickly in frustration.

Personally, I would have preferred not to come but I really would do anything for Harrison. We might have lost three years but I didn't want to waste any more time.

Turning my head slightly, I looked at him to see he was equally frustrated by the sound and fools in the crowd. I subtly squeezed his hand to comfort him. Enjoying the warmth and rough feel of his hands. I didn't want this to end as I remembered our summer evenings together as friends when we would just talk and enjoy each others' company. Almost like we were the only two people in the world. Despite that being when Harrison was straight I still loved those times and I was determined to have those moments again. Regardless of religious haters and our autistic difficulties.

Then I turned my attention back to the crowd.

As I studied the fools in the crowd, I clocked people moving and walking towards the stage.

I looked at Alessandria. She was looking at the ceiling.

I knew something was wrong but even I knew social convention said I couldn't shout without proof.

Narrowing my eyes, I focused on the crowd. My dulled blade slowed in my hands as I focused.

I let go of Harrison's warm hand and I carefully moved my hand down my leather cloak to my waist. And my covertly sheathed sword.

The crowd got louder as the Queen finished.

I tensed.

People were shouting.

Alessandria shouted and a shot was fired.

I looked at Harrison. He was fine.

Chaos unfolded as people flee and the guards formed a wall around the Queen.

My mind ran as the noises and screams became too much.

My dulled blade span rapidly.

I felt Harrison rub my leather cloaked shoulders.

Twenty voices screamed as one something about a triad.

My mind cleared as I remembered my duty. The Queen and Alessandria but most of all Harrison were in danger.

I saw twenty black cloaked figures advance.

The air stunk of sweat and fear.

I whipped out my long black longsword.

My sister ran off the stage.

Nemesio ran to the Queen.

Charging into the crowd, I joined Alessandria.

People ran and screamed.

I knocked them to the side.

The black cloaked figures whipped out two long black swords as one.

Their timing was almost supernatural.

Hellen ran past me. Whacking one of the cloaked men with her big stick.

I ran to her.

Thrusting my sword through his chest.

Two other men charged at us.

Hellen used her stick to meet the sword blows.

I blocked the incoming swords.

Before jumping to the left. The man felt forward. I kicked him in the back.

He fell.

Hellen whacked him over the head.

His skull cracked.

Blood and brain matter pouring out.

Fast air rushed past me.

I spun around.

The other man swung at me and Hellen.

She hit the man's swords. I split his throat with a single swing.

More men came.

More gunshots were fired.

Everyone was gone.

The military, church, and everyone else had fled.

Cowards!

We were outnumbered.

More assassins charged at us.

"To me!" Alessandria screamed behind me.

We complied.

I swung my swords again as more assassins came.

Before we ran to the stage.

Hellen and I joined Alessandria in creating a line in front of the stage.

The smell of fear and sweat only grew.

The twelve remaining assassins charged.

Their swords swinging.

Alessandria artfully dodged out of the way.

Two men came flying past.

Hellen thrusted her big stick into the back of one man.

His back cracked. He screamed.

The other man flew past me. I forced my sword through his left eye.

Blood squirted out.

I heard Harrison give a shocked sound. I didn't care.

A sword sliced my upper arm.

I screamed.

Pain flooded me from new and old wounds alike.

Another hit made me drop my sword.

I spun around.

A black cloaked female stood there.

I charged.

She tried to strike me down.

Jumping around, I dodged the strikes.

I pounced on her.

My fists smashed into her face repeatedly.

Her bones shattered.

Her blood sprayed up my arms and face.

Her skin split. Letting her bones and blood pour out.

I picked up my sword.

Alessandria grabbed me.

I tensed but I saw nine cloaked men storming towards us.

Suddenly, the door on the far side of the

chamber exploded open.

Military soldiers poured in.

Firing rifle after rifle.

The black cloaked men turned.

We didn't hesitate.

We all lunged forward.

Letting our swords rip into the flesh of our attackers.

Within moments, the attackers were dead, and the chamber was painted in the blood and flesh of our enemies.

Looking at Alessandria and Hellen, we all smiled. It was great fighting with them, and I have to confess fighting is one of the few times I feel emotion.

Then I looked at the other time I feel emotion, Harrison gave me a half-heartened smile. I couldn't blame him. He probably had no idea what he just witnessed.

Yet I have more pressing concerns as I walked over to Alessandria who was inspecting the dead.

"We were lucky today," Alessandria stated plainly.

I was about to speak when a large muscular man stormed over in heavy smelly armour and demanded in a rough voice: "Your Majesty speak to me!"

Alessandria and I both looked at each other. Our day got even more interesting.

CHAPTER 5

Alessandria looked away from the corpse as she turned her attention to the large muscular man who walked towards the stage and the Queen.

She frowned as she focused on the man's black heavy armour and all his shiny medals of various acts of bravery and impressive kills. Probably meaning other people did the acts but he took the credit. From her military days, Alessandria knew how these higher ups worked.

Nevertheless, Alessandria knew exactly who the man was as his heavy footsteps chipped the stone floor and echoed off the immense stone walls. Even the sun through the stained glass windows seemed to dim as the man came closer.

Of all the men to storm in here after an attack, Alessandria really didn't want the Head of the Military here. Despite him sending plenty of business in her family's direction, he wasn't exactly pleasant. And that was before she remembered his attitude towards people who never served or had left Military service.

The man's rough features scanned the room. Looking at the bodies. Alessandria guessed he thought he was in a war zone. Perhaps she would have preferred that as she smelt his disgusting whiskey that filled the chamber. Even her expensive fruity perfume couldn't compete with that horrific smell. A foul taste of cheap alcohol filled her mouth.

Then she remembered the rumours of his tendencies to get stone drunk every night. Casting her memories back to her mother, Alessandria understood why Kinaaz had gone to rehab in the countryside. Herself and Daniel supported her of course since this took courage. But they didn't think she needed it with being a highly functioning alcoholic.

However, seeing this Head of the Military, she appreciated and loved her mother a bit more. Knowing she wanted to improve her life before she got to this state.

Walking over to the stage, Alessandria saw the guards step away with their immense red shields. Allowing the Queen in her still sterile white dress to walk towards the Military Leader.

Alessandria noticed the guards were tensed and Daniel picked up his dulled blade and walked over as well.

Slowly, it began to dawn on Alessandria that the Military was in charge of security today and she had no idea how the assassins had come in.

Nemesio started to walk towards the Military Leader but she waved him back. Knowing how distressed Daniel got around him. She needed to talk to him later to see how his therapy was going.

Turning her attention back to the military leader, Alessandria noticed his swords and pistols on his waist. They were certainly more practical than ceremonial. And odd considering he's in the palace. So why did he keep such weapons?

"You! Your Majesty, you will listen to me!" the man screamed in a rough tone.

The Queen smiled and gracefully walked over to us.

Her white dress elegantly flowing across the cold stone floor as she moved.

The Guards followed close behind.

"I do not have to do anything, dear Ares. I have refused audience with you before and I shall do so now. Be gone,"

"You will regret this Queen,"

"Watch your tongue," Alessandria firmly said.

"This Queen will ruin us!"

Daniel whipped out his sword and pointed it at the man's throat.

Alessandria couldn't blame her brother. Then she smiled as Ares made his next mistake.

He knocked the sword aside and grabbed Daniel.

Daniel screamed.

Pushing Ares' hands away before diving on him. Smashing his fists into his face.

Alessandria nor the Queen was going to stop him.

The Dominicus Procurator even thought she

saw the Queen smile.

"Daniel enough," Harrison said as he walked over.

Daniel's ears picked at the sound of Harrison's voice and he begruntling complied.

Harrison stopped next to Daniel and sneered at Ares.

"Ha. You freaks are just lap dogs for one another,"

Harrison punched Ares' in the nose. Breaking it. Blood poured from the shattered nose.

Ares went for Harrison.

"Enough!" Alessandria commanded.

Ares backed down but spat at Daniel.

"I would be less concerned about Daniel Fireheart if I was you," the Queen coldly stated. "You were in charge of security today. Look around you. Assassins lay dead at my feet. Assassins that never should have been here,"

"Your majesty, this is clearly the work of Mortisical. Correct your mistake and let's fight them,"

Alessandria rolled her eyes as she looked at a male corpse with fair tanned skin and well-kept features.

"The Queen made no mistake. These men lack the purple taint in their skin that Mortisicals do,"

Ares spat at Alessandria.

Daniel's dulled blade spun faster.

"Harrison please take Daniel to his quarters. Daniel, I will speak with you later,"

Both Harrison and Daniel nodded.

As they walked away, Daniel shouted: "I rejected your military contract *Lord* Ares,"

The Guards slammed the doors behind Daniel and Harrison.

"What contract?" the Queen bit.

Alessandria noticed the Guards tensing.

"Your majesty that freak is lying,"

"My brother does not lie,"

"Fine then I asked the freak to acquire food supplies, ships, men and weapons for us,"

"I did not order this or sign any contract of this kind,"

"But you will your majesty, the Mortisical and our neighbours are growing in power. We must fight back or face extinction,"

The Queen stepped towards him.

"I am Queen. I am Sovereign. You shall not make their decisions based on fear and faulty logic. I have intelligence services and they have found no evidence of this. The only reason you still stand with your head attached to your shoulders is due to your past service to my father,"

Ares's hands formed fists.

The Queen smiled almost daring him to attack her.

In all honesty, Alessandria would have loved to see the outcome. Who would kill him first? The Queen? Her? Or the Guards?

Ares spat on the floor and stormed out.

CHAPTER 6

I allowed the weighted sheets to mould to my body as I laid back. Feeling the smooth weighted materials under me as I thought about the stupidity of what was going on.

After the Queen ordered the Military contract to be cancelled and words being spoken with the Head of the Military, Harrison escorted me back to my room and, I suppose, sadly he left for work.

Looking around my new bedroom in the castle, I realised it was rather good considering this use to be for Queen's personal guards.

Well, I have a large bed with weighted sheets to comfort me and a boring looking wardrobe and small desk. It's not the fanciest and I do realise I need to get some more personalised items. But at least I have a bunch of beautiful purple, red and blue flowers on top of the desk that Harrison bought me.

Personally, I hate flowers but these were pleasant to look at and at least they made the room smell of honey and citrus.

Anyway, I shook my head as I realised I was only letting my mind think about this because I didn't want to think about the idea of Nemesio coming up with Alessandria. Then I looked at my dulled blade and I hadn't realised it was spinning so fast in my hand.

Taking a few deep breaths, I tried to think about the therapy sessions, I've been attending after the whole Flesheater situation. But that only annoyed me more.

This whole thing was annoying. How dare some assassins try to kill Alessandria, the Queen and Harrison.

Yet I have to admit there something strange about that Military leader, something and me Alessandria needed to find out.

The only bit of comfort I got from the attack today was I managed to get out of that horrible social situation. All those noises and people were awful. It was all too much. The noise, no no, no. It was all too much. I hate being around that many people!

A few moments later, the large wooden door slowly opened and Alessandria walked in.

Thankfully she was alone and I appreciated the fact she opened the door quietly.

Sitting back up on my bed, I smiled at her as I saw her strong black metal armour and brown cloak.

She passed me a damp cloth. As I wiped my face, partly hating the damp feeling of the cloth against my skin. I laughed briefly as I forgot the blood was still on my face.

"You okay?" she asked.

"I must thank you for making me go. I never liked that Ares' character,"

"I don't think many people do. Where's

Harrison?"

Deciding that I had to smile at the question, I replied: "It turns out, we both forget people outside the Nobility have to work real jobs,"

Alessandria gave a nod of agreement.

"Daniel, what can you tell me about the contract?"

Digging into my trench coat, I pulled out the contract and passed it to her.

Alessandria unfolded the contract.

"Wait, he wanted a lot of ships and men,"

Her eyes widened as she read the price, he was going to pay us.

"He couldn't have expected us to sign this off. Not without at least the Queen's signature,"

"My theory is he thought we have commoners do all our work like the other Nobles Houses," I suggested.

"And a commoner would have presumed this was normal?"

"It's logical,"

Alessandria nodded.

"What about the food supplies, Daniel? He must know we don't have control over them,"

Now, I had to smile because that comment just shows how little the rest of my family knows about how we make our money, and the legal powers we're granted.

"Incorrect, dear sister," I lent closer towards her. "Whilst the Greenscales are the Nobles who have control over the food industry. If we need rations for the military, I can and normally write a formal request and they normally grant it. Or I can invoke legal powers to make them give us the rations,"

Alessandria nodded her head in surprise.

"Why do you ask?"

"Well, Daniel. Ares must have some sort of backup plan if he wants his rogue crusade to happen. How else could he get the rations without raising too many eyebrows?"

Now, I had to think about it. Spinning my dulled blade slowly in my hand, I thought about how I would gather secret rations.

"Alessandria, he would have more legal powers than me. He could force the Greenscales to provide him with the supplies without going through any sort of court,"

"You know the Greenscales Daughter, right?"

"Albania. We're still friends and she does have a great knowledge of military history,"

"Good to hear. At least you have someone else to talk about your limited interests with,"

I nodded with a bit of delight. As much as I don't like people, I did enjoy Albania's company. Especially, when her family found some ancient war object in the fields. I remember a lot of great evenings with her.

"I'll go and see her for you,"

"Thank you, and one last thing, if I may?"

Of course, I knew she was going to ask about

Nemesio but she wanted to be nice, so I supposed I needed to play along.

"What?"

"Why are you still avoiding Nemesio? Hasn't he proved himself yet?"

I shuffled across the bed to sit closer to her. As I breathed in her sweet perfume, I replied:

"I am getting there. Please just be patient. I'm still coming to terms with what he caused, and I still wake up screaming most nights at the nightmares,"

She slowly nodded her head and looked to the floor. Clearly, ashamed of bringing it up. I didn't have the heart to tell her my arms often feel like they're burning from my own wounds and the wounds inflicted upon me during my torture sessions.

Against my better judgement, I slowly and awkwardly hugged her. Focusing on the good I was doing her and ignoring my hate for contact.

Feeling her smile, I replied: "If you let go, I'll try and get the Greenscales to pledge support to you?"

Alessandria gently hit me and let go.

CHAPTER 7

Staring out the window of Hellen's office since her office was unavailable apparently, Alessandria looked out over the stunning castle grounds to see the lunch crowd walking into the city to eat and drink at the local cafes.

Memories of the busy loud streets packed with life and laughter made Alessandria smile and desperate to go out soon for a fun night with Hellen.

Even the thought of eating and drinking out made her mouth water and sweet meaty tastes form on her tongue.

Pulling her attention away from her food fantasies, Alessandria looked at her clear neat wooden desk with only a pile of folders on it. Then she looked at Hellen's desk. It was a symphony of chaos as piles were knocked over and stains of tea painted the documents.

Alessandria loved her friend but she needed to be more organised. Yet Alessandria couldn't understand why she had to share an office with Hellen. She was a Dominucus Procurator, so surely she would share an office with her equal who looked over the Crowd's land?

Shaking her head, Alessandria moved away from the window as she felt the beaming sun through the window start to burn her skin.

Looking around, Alessandria acknowledged the dull cream stone walls and thought about getting some paint and artwork. At least it would add some colour and character to the room. One of the reasons Alessandria hated doing all her Dominicus Procurator work was because she felt as if the room sucked the life from her. Even the silence now in the office felt wrong and creepy.

Shaking the negative thoughts away, Alessandria wandered over to Hellen's desk, her feet tapping gently on the floor, and she started to flick through the files.

Although, the concerning thing was each file she moved kicked up the smell of damp orange and lemon from Hellen's tea. Making Alessandria concerned that Hellen had spilt her drink on them. Where the files ruined?

She really didn't want to find out so Alessandria rushed back over to her desk and looked at the small clock she had on there. As she looked at the time, her stomach knotted at the thought of Nemesio being gone for over an hour. What if the contact he was seeing had hurt him?

Whilst her feelings were mixed towards him with flashes of affection washing over her from time to time. She still didn't want anything bad to happen to him. Or at least too bad after what he caused Daniel to go through.

After a few moments, Nemesio walked into

the office wearing his blue and fiery red armour. He smiled at her.

"I take it things didn't go perfectly with your contact?"

"They went just fine,"

"Did he give us anything useful?"

Nemesio shrugged and took a few steps closer to Alessandria.

"I'm not sure, but what do we know about these assassins?"

Alessandria stepped away from Nemesio and paced around in the office.

"We know they were in the crowd. They would have had to pass at least five checkpoints,"

"Really?"

"Well Nemesio that's if we presume, they sneaked in as guests,"

"Unlikely, the guests had to be searched by Order of the Queen. Only people she personally invited didn't have to be searched. Like us and Daniel,"

"What about Hellen and the other security people?"

"As far as I know they weren't searched or checked,"

"Who appoints?" Alessandria asked.

"Ares was in charge of security, so it had to be him,"

Alessandria allowed a small smile to break her serious expression as she remembered Hellen's shocked expression at being summoned by the grumpy Ares.

"Nemesio, how would Ares get twenty assassins in the castle?"

Nemesio shook his head slowly.

"Hypothetically, one of my jobs in the Inquisition was to examine places and find all weak points,"

"And let me guess hypothetically, it's easy to sneak people and supplies into the castle?"

"Yes,"

Alessandria made a note of that on her desk to make sure these weak points were strengthened. Anything to protect her family... and the Queen, of course.

"Okay. Someone in security was involved, but who were the attackers? The Procurators say they were hired blades,"

"I agree. My contact added they were probably in the employ of The Serpent Guild,"

"Really? The Serpent Guild?"

"Yes, you know the biggest criminal gang in Ordericous. You must know them as a Dominicus Procurator?"

"I have heard of them, but they stay away from Fireheart Land. I've never investigated them, but I hear they're great at controlling the underworld,"

Nemesio nodded.

"Wait, doesn't the Inquisition have some sort

of agreement with them?"

The Former Inquisitor's face paled.

"Not the Inquisition per say. The Order of the Sacred Fire, before we thankfully destroyed it, did have an agreement. Saying they must inform us of all activity, or we would slaughter them and burn their families alive,"

Alessandria's eyes widened and she nodded. Even after seeing the extremes of the Inquisitorial Order, Alessandria was still amazed at the horrors and butchery the Inquisition was prepared to commit in the name of their so-called divine missions.

"Any other Orders?"

"No, the Guilds tend to stay away from the Inquisitorial Orders,"

"For good reasons?"

Nemesio smiled and nodded.

Looking around to see if she had forgotten anything, Alessandria headed towards the door and said: "Right then, let's go and see the Head of The Serpent's Guild,"

Nemesio touched her back quickly.

Alessandria wished he would do more.

"Alessandria, your brother. Does he still hate me?"

Slowly, she turned to face him. Seeing the conflict and sadness in his eyes. Maybe he did truly regret his actions?

"Hate is a strong word. He is trying. Give him time and he might forgive you. But you must remember what you did to him, or what you caused,"

Nemesio's eyes fell to the floor.

"I hate myself every day for what I caused him to go through,"

Alessandria rubbed his hands briefly.

He seemed to smile at her touch.

"Give him time,"

CHAPTER 8

As the cold coffee touched my lips, an explosion of chocolatey notes filled my taste buds with the bitter taste of the coffee.

Lowering the mug, I carefully placed it back on the small circular table in front of me and did one of my favourite activities- people watching. Whilst I played with my dulled blade in my hand.

Looking to my left I peaked down at the crowds of people in the dirt filled street as they hurried about their afternoon business. Some in their brown work clothes rushed to deliver goods and complete their Master's jobs. Others in their assortment of colours leisurely and rather pointlessly strolled about visiting the various shops on either side of the street.

Now, I might hate people and especially pointless people but I do appreciate people are fascinating.

Rising my head to look at this rooftop garden of the coffee shop, it was thankfully empty with a few rows of small tables with parchment menus on them.

A waitress walked past and winked at me. I rolled my eyes.

The distinctive smell of bitter coffee and sweet cakes filled my nose as steam jetted out of a nearby vent. Normally, I would hate the feeling of the warm steam but the smell of coffee made it tolerable.

Finishing off my coffee, I looked down at the street again to see if Albania was coming. Sure, the messenger confirmed she was attending this urgent meeting but the Greenscales weren't exactly the most punctual of families. Which did have its comedy value. Especially, when the Greenscales were meant to come out with us one day and they were three hours late.

Although, I have to confess I hate late people. Hate it with a passion. How hard is it to arrive on time? It isn't.

Hearing more footsteps coming towards me, I looked over and smiled as Albania came towards me. In all fairness, she was on time. I was just extremely early.

As Albania came towards me, I appreciated her good dress sense with her light bluish-green dress that flowed in the light breeze and her strong long blond hair blow gently in the wind.

She gracefully sat down and a waitress came over with two cups of black coffee and a slice of a sickly chocolate cake for Albania. She nodded her thanks.

After Albania cleared her throat, she elegantly said "We were certainly surprised to receive your letter, Daniel Fireheart. We believed your House was destroyed and the Queen only acted out of pity,"

My eyes narrowed.

"Now, now dearest Albania. How long did your father make you practice that paragraph?"

She nodded and cocked her head.

"It is good to see you once more, Daniel. How are things at the castle?"

Now, Daniel cocked his head. Why was his old friend being so formal and distant?

"Albania, you know I don't do chit chat. So I ask you why are you being so… different and quite frankly annoying?"

The Daughter of the Greenscales raised her hands and rested her face in them.

"I'm sorry, Daniel. It's work and everything. I've not had a normal person to talk to for ages,"

"I do not class myself as normal, but I'll forgive you for that oversight,"

I continued to play with my dulled bladed as Albania slipped her coffee.

"Has the military come to you recently?" I asked.

Albania coughed and choked on her coffee.

"Um, no,"

"Do not lie to me my friend. The military wants rations. Your family controls the entire food supply in Ordericous. They came to you,"

Albania nodded and looked around.

My eyes narrowed at her concern. Did she really think she would be followed?

Leaning in closer, Daniel asked: "What's going on?"

"My father and Mother are being kept under house arrest and I am having to deal with Ares and his goonies. They have sieged all our yield for the year. Ordericous will starve in a matter of months,"

I nodded.

"Our farms are being patrolled by soldiers and our own military detachment has turned against us. Our people are slaving away in the fields,"

"Do they know you are here?"

Albania paused.

"That's the weird thing. They wanted me to come here. They demanded it. I wanted to stay and protect my people, but they wanted me gone,"

"Did they give you a message?"

"No, they just said to tell you everything. There's nothing you can do,"

I leaned back in my chair. Allowing the warm afternoon sun to heat my skin. I smiled at the arrogance of the military. Did they really think the House of Fireheart was weak and powerless against their plot to raise an illegal army and kill the Queen? The sheer ignorance of the idea was laughable.

"So, you're telling me the military has seized your land and taken you all prisoner?"

"Yes, but it's all legal,"

Thinking about her last comment, I knew she was right. It was within Ares' power to do all these things. Of course, using the legal powers to this extent hadn't been done in over a thousand years. Yet it was all legal. Nonetheless, Alessandria needed to hear this.

"Albania, do you want your land back?"

She looked confused.

"Yes! Those are my people. It is my duty to protect them and make money from them,"

"Alessandria and I will free your land for a price?"

"Don't be stupid Daniel,"

My dulled blade spun faster.

"You cannot free my land. Your House isn't powerful enough,"

"Do not concern yourself with the method. But we want something in exchange?"

"Fine. I doubt this will cost me anything. What do you desire then?"

Looking her dead in the eye before I remembered how much I hate eye contact, I firmly said: "Alessandria wants to change the law about gays becoming Lords of Noble Houses. When her legal change comes to the vote, we want your House's unquestioning support,"

She busted out laughing.

"Wow, the House of Fireheart really has lost itself. That will never get to court. The legal change will be rejected,"

"As I said leave the method to us,"

"Fine. You'll never be able to get my land back but if you do, sure. We will support your legal change on our honour,"

"Thank you,"

Having enough of her negative words, I stood up, fought the urge to throw her drink over her nice dress and I walked away. Ready to prove her wrong.

CHAPTER 9

With four men either side of them gladded in thick heavy metal armour, Nemesio and Alessandria walked into a great chamber deep under Ordericous.

Looking around Alessandria sneered at the chamber at its ugliness as it was cruelly carved out from the various cave systems under the country.

Yet the tunnels of the cave system were cold dark and damp with the constant sound of dripping water. Not the nicest of places to rule the criminal underworld from.

Nevertheless, Alessandria knew this criminal gang leader must have enjoyed it. Judging by the hundreds of rotting corpses at the entrance of the caves. She recognised some of them from gangers she had arrested over the years.

Whilst, Alessandria might not have placed them at the entrance to warn off other criminals and Procurators. She always appreciated people with flare and character.

A constant dripping sound filled the chamber as a new crack appeared in the cave ceiling and more water dripped down. Making the already damp floor considerably worse. This couldn't be healthy.

The hairs on Alessandria's arms stuck up as a freezing breeze rushed past. She would love to be above ground in the sun again.

Heavy footsteps banged on the damp bedrock as the guards left the chamber. Alessandria's eyebrows rose at the oddity of it. It was odd enough Nemesio had managed to schedule an urgent meeting with this leader at short notice. But for them to be left alone in the heart of their operation. That seemed even odder.

With the smell of damp mould filling her nostrils, Alessandria really wanted to be above ground. But her typical and probably stubborn sense of duty made her drawn to this smelly cave.

Slowly, Nemesio crept over to her and Alessandria smiled as she felt his warm body heat radiate towards her. Her arm hairs lowered themselves. She wondered how hot his skin was.

A pair of shuffling feet dragged themselves across the cave behind them.

Turning around, Alessandria clocked her head and narrowed her eyes at the sight of an elderly fragile woman shuffling towards them.

Alessandria didn't know what to focus on first. The fact this criminal leader was a fragile old lady or her bright blue dress. That really didn't do much for her. Alessandria was pretty sure it made her look even older. At least the old lady wore strong flowery perfume. It certainly improved the smell!

In an overexcited voice, the old lady shrieked: "Oh dearest Nemmy you return!"

The old lady shuffled over and tightly hugged Nemesio.

Alessandria's eyebrows rose.

"You two know each other?"

"Oh of course we do! This man, my Nemmy, well he is a great man. He killed all my competition for me,"

Alessandria cocked her head.

"Oh Nemmy, who is this beautiful lady? Just look at her. Simply stunning,"

Nemesio only smiled at Alessandria. Was he agreeing?

"Oh Nemmy say something,"

Slowly, Nemesio spoke: "There was a mission in the Inquisition to replace the head of the criminal underworld with a more... suitable leader,"

"And that's her?"

"Oh of course. I'm a treasure really. As Nemmy will tell you. I only kill you if you cross me. But I'm sure if Nemmy is your friend, you'll be fine,"

Alessandria had no idea what to say. She had too many questions. Why name him Nemmy?

"I am Alessandria Fireheart, Dominicus Procurator for the House of Fireheart. It is a pleasure to meet you, and thank you for not operating on my family's land,"

As a gesture of good faith and to remove temptation when her mother returned, Alessandria passed the old lady the finest bottle of wine the Firehearts owned.

"Oh Nemmy, look! Look! Oh, this will look fabulous in my collection. Oh, she is wonderful

Nemmy. Let me fine a Guard," the old lady said as she shuffled towards the door.

Alessandria stood close to Nemesio and asked: "Please explain,"

Nemesio smiled and looked in her eyes.

"The Inquisition needed to find a person to look after the criminal underworld. A person who would stop anything major from happening. So I was sent undercover and I made sure she rise to power,"

"Nemmy?"

"She's a bit eccentric,"

"Only slightly,"

The shuffling sounds of the old lady returned as she shuffled towards them.

"Oh Nemmy, I know ya don't come here to see me. Why ya here Nemmy?"

Nemesio gestured over to Alessandria.

"Oh Nemmy, you don't need to ask my blessing to marry her. She's a Fireheart, a good family. And just look at her. She's fabulous,"

Alessandria smiled without knowing why.

"No, Serpent. She needs to talk to you,"

"Oh, why didn't ya say so?"

The old lady shuffled over to Alessandria.

"If my Nemmy talks to you then so can I. What's up?"

"Um, thank you. This morning there was an attack on the Queen,"

"No, not Queeny. My Queeny been good to me over the years. Ya know not sending in the soldiers. How can I help my Queeny?"

"The men that attacked were hired guns, well-trained, well-armed and wore black cloaks. There was a woman there too. Do you know these people?"

The old lady shuffled away and circled herself a few times.

"Oh Nemmy, your girl is clever, very clever. She remembered the woman. You wouldn't have. The men I don't know but the woman and the black cloaks. I know them. I know who hired them,"

"Great, who?"

The old lady's face changed from overexcitement to something more serious. She shuffled over to Alessandria.

"I'll make ya a deal. I'll give ya the name of the person who hired them. And the underworld support on ya law change. If ya do something for me,"

Immediately, Alessandria wanted to scream and shout an agreement. She needed all the support she could get, and it wouldn't surprise her if the underworld could bring some of the other Noble Houses in line. But she hated to think the cost.

"What's the catch?"

"Ah as my Nemmy will you. I'm a great deal maker. I'm honourable too. If you get my grandson released from the Queen's Court, he's on trial, you can have your name and my support. It's all on my honour. Nemmy can vouch for me,"

Nemesio nodded.

Alessandria wanted to say no. She didn't want to free a criminal but freeing one life for the sake of her Queen, was it worth it?

It didn't matter at the end of the day, Alessandria was duty bound to her Queen and someone was lying to her. Someone within the castle was involved. She had to find out no matter the cost.

"I agree to your terms,"

CHAPTER 10

I was hardly impressed as a woman led me into Ares' office. It was awful. The stone blocks that made up the box room were all chipped and cracked. The wall behind the desk, if you want to call it that, was covered in dripping water. Assuming a pipe had busted. And as for the desk, it was nothing more than a wooden table with some parchment on it. Hardly what I would have excepted from the Chief of the Military!

The iron door slammed shut behind me as the woman left without saying a word. Now, I understood what my secretary said that Ares' people being rude and awful.

On the way up I mentioned the tattoo on her hand from her squad. She shouted at me about the fact I know nothing about honourable service and I should shut up. It took all my willpower not to thrust my sword into her chest!

Noticing the bitter smell of beer mixed with the disgusting smell of chocolatey wine and a fruity taste developing in my mouth. I walked over behind the desk, hating the sound of footsteps echoing as I walked, to find easily twenty bottles of beer and wine there.

I suppose I understood now why mother went to rehab before she needed to. She was always good and cunning like that. A part of me smiled at the realisation she probably went to rehab to make sure she could continue scheming into her old age. Hell, she's probably scheming our return to power!

As I played with my dulled blade, I thought about what I would say to this fool. I had no power but I might be able to find something interesting. But I really wanted to get home to Harrison.

The iron door scratched across the stone floor as it opened and Ares stumbled in. Wearing a horrifically short robe. He smelt of awful beer. I wanted to vomit. I know it was 5 o'clock in the evening but still!

"What do you want freak?"

I rolled my eyes at having to deal with this man.

"Your siege of the Greenscales' land. End it now!"

"Never, dishonourable thing,"

"I am hardly dishonourable,"

"You do not serve. You do not continue to serve. You turned your back on the military,"

Again, I rolled my eyes at the stupidity and pointlessness of this man. This is one of the reasons why I hate people. Some of them are just so pointless.

"If that is your opinion so be it. Why did you siege their land?"

"We both know it is within my powers. You

can go to a judge or the Queen's Dominicus Procurator, but you will fail. They have no power to overrule me,"

I hate it when they know the law as well as I do.

My dulled blade span quicker.

"Why exactly siege it? You have no soldiers. Where would the food go?"

"I can and will siege whatever land I can,"

"Why?"

"That's classified and none of your business,"

"One call to the Queen and she will declare you a traitor,"

"And she will deal with the consequences,"

"Is that a threat, Ares?"

His hands started shaking a little. Whatever alcohol he drank was hopefully starting to take effect. I hope it starts to loosen his tongue.

"No, no threat, freak and where's your boyfriend? He will not protect you this time so get out of my office and leave me,"

"Not without you telling me the truth. I will get to the heart of these lies,"

"Daniel, I am not lying to you when I say this, abandon the Queen if you know what is good for you,"

"Why attack her?"

"I am not the one attacking the Queen. I just know things. Do yourself, your family and your freakish boyfriend a favour and abandon the Queen,"

"I will not!"

Ares fell to the floor and started snoring.

I rolled my eyes. He passed out from the drink.

The door exploded open.

I span around.

Five men in black cloaks and swords in both hands walked in.

The air stunk of urine and sweat.

They slammed the door shut.

I whipped out my sword.

They charged.

I dodge the swings.

Leaping onto the desk, I kicked the parchment at them.

It blinded one man.

I jumped.

Kicking him to the floor.

His head cracked on the stone floor. Watering the ground with his blood.

The other men charged.

I met three blades with my sword.

Another blade lightly cut my arm.

My old arm wounds screamed.

I bit back the pain.

They swung again.

I dived out the way.

A hand grabbed me.

I screamed as loud as I could.

I hear the whipping of a sword.

Falling to the ground, I dodged it.

Jumping back up, I punched one of the men.

His nose broke.

My hand was warm and wet with his blood.

A sword tapped my forearm.

Blood dripped from it.

Another man kicked me.

I screamed as my mind spun.

I needed to kill.

I needed to rip into their flesh.

The door busted open.

A blur of blue and fiery red armour came through.

The men paused.

I didn't hesitate.

I grabbed my sword.

Thrusting it into the enemy.

Blood sprayed up the walls.

Blood sprayed all over me as I hacked the enemy a part.

The blue and red blur joined me.

Hacking the head of another man, I knew there was only one man left.

I stared at him.

His black cloak wet with the blood of his friends.

A hand grabbed my shoulder, I screamed.

Smashing my fists in the person who touched me.

I saw the cloaked man move.

I didn't want him to escape.

Darting over to him, I sunk my nails into his flesh. Ripping chunks out until someone grabbed me.

Again, I screamed.

The blue and red blur killed the last man.

My vision cleared.

It was Nemesio and the blue and red fiery armour of the Inquisition.

I screamed in agony.

Not again.

Not the Inquisition.

Not the torturers.

I wanted to attack but... my body collapsed to a blackness without dreams.

CHAPTER 11

Alessandria simply sat back in her sterile white metal chair as she stared at Daniel. The heartache still pained her as she replayed how Nemesio had come running to her with Daniel's unconscious and bleeding body.

Alessandria shook her head at the terror of the situation and the terror of not knowing what happened.

Although, when the nurses undressed and washed all the blood off Daniel, Alessandria did have to smile as two of the nurses screamed when they saw Daniel's arms, and all the curved and somewhat artful wounds.

Now she just sat there, watching for her brother to wake up. The nurses were good by giving Daniel a room to himself. Yet Alessandria looked around the sterile white box room that stunk of harsh chemicals and she could still feel the water on the floor where the nurses had washed the room.

None of it mattered in the end though as Alessandria stared at Daniel in the hospital bed with the white linen sheet down by his waist. Revealing all his stab wounds on his chest from the Inquisition and all the wounds on his arms.

She knew he was a tortured soul, both literally and metaphorically, but she still loved her brother. Alessandria had thought about summoning Harrison but she didn't want to worry him. Or the real reason was because she just wanted this moment to be a sister. Not a Procurator, not a Fireheart, not anything just a sister that loves her brother.

An odd tapping sound outside the room reminded Alessandria, Hellen was outside. As much as she would love to have her friend with her. Alessandria didn't need Hellen staring at Daniel's one might say impressive muscles and abs.

Anyway, Alessandria needed to find out what was going on with Daniel and there were some things Hellen didn't need to know.

Stretching out her neck, Alessandria felt the cold night air starting to set in as it started to cool her skin and the metal chair slightly.

Hearing the sheets rustling, Alessandria looked at Daniel to see him weakly smiling at her.

"What happened?" he asked and started to search around for his dulled blade.

Alessandria placed it in his hand, and he started playing with it.

"You tell me. I was about to talk to Lord Justice and the next moment Nemesio came running with your unconscious body,"

Daniel flinched at the sound of Nemesio's name.

"Daniel, the doctors said you collapsed from exhaustion after your attack. When did you last sleep?"

Daniel smiled a little and said: "The real question is when did I last sleep well,"

Alessandria leaned in closer.

"I haven't slept well since I was taken. Every night I wake up screaming as the memories of the torture comes back. Every night my cold sweat covers the bed. Every night Harrison has to comfort me,"

Alessandria didn't speak. What could she say?

"I'm... sorry. How's therapy going?"

Daniel played with his dulled blade more.

"The doctors are good. I'll give them that. But we've hit a wall now,"

"Why?"

"The doctors want me to experience desensitisation so I'm not as fearful of the Inquisition and to dull my heightened survival instincts. It's a sound idea. But I'm too fearful. I almost killed the doctor when he wore the symbol of the Order,"

Alessandria opened her mouth to say something but there was nothing she could say. She couldn't even begin to imagine what the Inquisition had done to him. Not just physical torture but mental torture too.

"Please, Daniel. Is there anything I can do?"

"Answer a question for me,"

"Anything,"

"Nemesio, do you find him attractive?"

A piece of cold sweat dripped down Alessandria's face. She didn't know, and what could she say to Daniel?

Of course, she could lie to him and completely deny it, but she wouldn't lie to her brother. If she admitted it, would he hate her?

"I don't know, Daniel. I'm sorry. I really don't know,"

Focusing on his dulled blade, Daniel smiled a little.

"It's fine. You can like or even love whoever you want. You have my blessing if you want to date him. At least you would be dating someone of status and not a commoner. I think that's how mother would put it,"

Without knowing why Alessandria beamed. Maybe she did find Nemesio attractive? Maybe she did want to be with him?

"Thank you, how is Harrison by the way?"

Daniel's eyes lit up.

"He's great. He is patient. I'll give him that. Does he know I'm here?"

"No,"

"Good, I'll tell him later and…"

"What, Daniel?"

"Can I ask you a personal question?"

Alessandria nodded if only out of curiosity.

"You're not a virgin are you?"

Alessandria's eyes widened at the type of conversation.

"Compared to Hellen, I am,"

Daniel smiled.

"Harrison wants us to do it. And I'm not sure about it?"

"Why not?"

"You know as an autistic person. I have a *mild* touch sensitivity,"

"Mild? More like severe but go on,"

"And I'm just concerned I won't enjoy it or I won't cope with it,"

Alessandria lent back in her cold chair. This was hardly her area of expertise. What if she gave him bad advice? What if he hated it?

Taking a deep breath, Alessandria calmly replied: "Daniel, Harrison loves you. You're both autistic. Just talk to him and he'll understand,"

Daniel nodded.

"Why were you seeing the Lord Justice?"

"Change the subject, why don't you. Um, we made a deal with the head of The Serpent Gang. We need to free her grandson,"

Daniel nodded.

"What about your attackers?"

"Same people who attacked the Queen. You're in a better position to peruse that line of inquiry,"

Alessandria couldn't argue with that, but she coughed as the smell of the medical chemicals entered her nose again.

"How did your meeting with the Greenscales go?"

"Good, they pledge their support to you if we

free their land from the military siege," Daniel started as he got out of bed and looked for his leather trench coat and trousers.

"What are you doing?"

"I need to go to the Queen's Procurator's Archives to find the legal basis for the siege. Even if it's within his power, he had to create a report,"

"Daniel, it's seven o'clock at night. You just collapsed from exhaustion,"

"I'll take Hellen with me,"

"I'm not going to persuade you otherwise, am I?"

"No. Whilst you and Nemesio go to see the Lord Justice, we'll search the archives. Come to Harrison's house afterwards. We'll regroup,"

Knowing her brother wasn't going to back down, Alessandria passed him his leather trench coat, sword and leather trousers. It only bought her some comfort that Hellen could protect him. She couldn't afford to lose him. Yet at least he said Nemesio's name without tensing.

CHAPTER 12

Despite my body aching and my head a tiny bit fuzzy from fatigue, myself and Hellen entered the Archive deep under the castle. In all honesty, I'm not sure if I'm aching from the fatigue or the ridiculously long spiralling staircase we had to walk down to get here.

The sound of Hellen's big wooden stick tapping against the dark stone floor thankfully broke the silence of being so deep below ground. I could probably scream in here and no one would be able to hear me.

Looking at Hellen with her massive stick and her grey Procurator cloak. I was definitely grateful Alessandria made me bring her. With her stick nearby, I felt a lot safer but something was still off.

As I looked at the immense books of parchment containing centuries worth of documents. The fact that there was only one light and a lot of hiding places didn't exactly make me feel comfortable down here.

Focusing on the Archive in more detail, I appreciate the bookshelves bolted to the walls. To support the immense weight of the centuries old brown leather book covers.

Hellen walked past me and looked behind the back of the bookshelf on the far end of the Archive. She shook her head and I knew why. From looking at a map of the archives a few years ago, I know this place is a maze and this little 'entrance' way with three bookcases and a small wooden table around us was only a fraction of the true inventory.

Thankfully, I doubt Ares would have been bothered to file the case correctly. Meaning it should theoretically be in this 'entrance' part.

However, I hate the smell of the Archive. All these dusty book covers and smelly ancient bits of parchment, most of which I'm sure were mouldy. Not exactly my scene. I love books but not smelly parchment.

Taking a few steps closer towards the wooden table, I cocked my head at the strange map laid out. It showed an ancient coastline of Mortisical. Surely Ares had wanted to see this for his rogue crusade. It's all rather stupid if you ask me. Attacking the Mortisicals is pointless and we've won anyway.

That's one of the benefits of having a boyfriend with personal access to the Queen. He got to proofread the final proof of the peace treaty and the Queen asked for his opinion as a common subject. Then he told me all of the details of the treaty. I don't know why Ares' is complaining we make a lot more money from this peace deal than at war. But what are you going to do with ignorant people?

Turning my attention to Hellen, she started to look at the cold leather book covers and I started to notice she was shivering in her Procurator cloak. I couldn't blame her it was approaching nine o'clock at night and it might be summer. But down here that didn't matter!

Stepping forward, I went to one of the bookcases and started to look at the large leather book covers. I wasn't looking at the covers. I needed to look at the dust on the bookshelves. Nobody ever comes down here so a book without a thick layer of dust in front of it was strange.

Hellen wandered over, tapping her big stick as she did, and she pointed to a book cover at the bottom.

Knowing I wasn't going to pick it up, Hellen rolled her eyes and picked it up. Her face pulled a drained expression. I couldn't blame her, the book looked to be over twenty kilograms. She dumped it on the wooden table that cracked a little under the weight.

"Thank you," I said as I threw the book cover open and started to page through it.

"What ya looking for?"

"Even if Ares knew no one would demand to see a legal justification of the Greenscales siege. He would have made one and that's what we're looking for,"

"Why put the doc in a book from two centuries ago? That sounds boring,"

"I don't think 200 year old legal cases are meant to be fun,"

"I donna know. I've seen some great 500-year-old cases. People did some creative murders back then,"

I simply nodded as I paged through more of the book.

"Don't ya just shake the book?"

She had a point. I could just lift up the two-hundred-year-old of book and see what falls out but knowing my luck everything would fall out.

Grabbing the edges of the book covers, I lifted up the book, fighting against the strain in my arms, and shook the book a few times. Three pieces of crystal white parchment fell on the floor.

Hellen picked them up and shook her head.

"These doesn't look like two-hundred-year-old parchment," she added as she passed me two sheets. "This all seems fine. This talks about the intelligence reports showing Mortisical amassing an army,"

Turning to Hellen, I laid out the three sheets of parchment on the wooden table and I pointed to each of the pairs of signatures on them.

Her eyes widened.

"I didn't think the Queen knew about the siege,"

"She doesn't, Hellen. These are fake. Someone faked the Queen's signature. Even some of these facts are wrong or bending of the truth. That report outlined in your sheet is the one I wrote three years ago,"

Hellen shook her head.

"This is all built on a bed of lies and deception. The men that Ares' controls are believing in lies," I explained.

Hellen was about to open her mouth when multiple footsteps came from the maze of the main archive.

She grabbed her stick.

I whipped out my sword. Its cold hilt in my hand.

Five females in dark cloaks walked out.

One immediately fired a crossbow at me.

It grazed my left shoulder.

Pain flooded my body.

The females advanced.

One woman charged at Hellen.

She thumped her with her stick. Then again and again.

Bones cracked and muscles ripped.

Another woman jumped at me. I slashed across her chest with my sword.

The crossbow fired again. Hitting my left arm.

The bolt radiated agony into my body. My arm felt as if it was on fire.

Hellen charged the women. Whacking her stick at them.

They punched her.

We looked at each other and nodded.

Hellen whacked the candle above the small wooden table.

It fell.

The two-hundred-year-old book caught ablaze.

Massive flames engulfed the table.

The women stumbled back.

We ran to the staircase.

As we reached it, a purple magical shield activated. Cutting the small 'entrance' off from the rest of the castle and archive.

I peeked at the women trapped inside.

The fire died out, but women looked as if they were screaming. Yet no sound came out as the magic in the archive sucked all the air out of the room. Choking the women to death.

My arm was wet with my blood and my arm pulsed with pain. I held my arm tight and bit my lip. Hopefully Alessandria and Nemesio were having better luck.

CHAPTER 13

Walking into the Lord Justice's office, Alessandria gasped immediately as she saw the entire chamber was like a small cathedral. With its large stained glass windows depicting former war heroes and gold leaf covering the walls of the domed room.

Equally, you could see the marks of walls where they had been damaged as the gold leaf was chipped or flaked off the walls. Yet Alessandria didn't care, this was beautiful. Even the floor was covered in a thick velvety red rug.

She took a few steps into the chamber just to feel the soft rug under her leather boots. It was like walking on air. Alessandria didn't want to leave.

This desire was further added to when she smelt the sweet citrus incense of sweet fruity oranges that burned on golden pillars in each of the four corners of the chamber.

Maybe she was tired but Alessandria could feel the excitement build within her. If the Lord Justice had an office this grand, what was the Queen's like?

Which was odd to Alessandria considering she had never been to the Queen's office or throne room. Maybe she needed to create an excuse to see it, and sit on the throne whilst she was there.

At the sound of someone moving in the office, Alessandria looked at the far end to see the Lord Justice getting up from his silver desk covered in piles of parchments and a golden sphere.

He smiled at her and he started to walk towards her in his long sterile white robes of office that draped across the floor behind him.

Despite Alessandria enjoying herself, maybe even too much, she almost sneered at how regal the Lord Justice was walking. He was no Queen. He was in charge of her so how dare he act superior in front of her.

Then she thought about it for a moment and as Lord Justice, all the Dominicus Procurators answered to him even the Queen's Dominicus Procurator. So maybe he was entitled to act superior. Alessandria gave a quick laugh at the silly thought.

Whilst Alessandria didn't mind the temperature of the office, she thought it was odd the office was so warm, warm enough she felt a drop of sweat down her back. Especially, since the wind of the ocean made summer nights pretty cold. Alessandria dismissed the train of thought as the Lord Justice came to meet her.

His old well-aged features smiled as he looked at Alessandria's youthful face. She returned the smile if not unsure about the reason for his smile. Nemesio thankfully came over to stand next to her.

The Lord Justice asked in a posh, elegantly almost lyrical voice "What do I own this unexpected pleasure, Lady Fireheart? It is a rare privilege to be graced by someone as legendary as you,"

"I did not know I was so legendary in the annuals of the procurators,"

"Lady Fireheart, you underestimate yourself. Few Procurators in our thousand-year history has taken down a Noble House,"

"You humble me, Lord Justice but I am not here for a social call,"

"That is a grand shame, my Lady. I would have appreciated the chance to pick such a fine and mighty brain,"

Alessandria wanted to take a step away from him, but she needed his help, unfortunately.

"Lord Justice, there is a prisoner awaiting to be tried for murder, drug possession and thievery in the Queen's Cells,"

"There are many such prisoners, my Lady. I politely request a name,"

"Danic Serpentine,"

The Lord Justice paused for a moment, his face allowing a puzzled expression to break his elegant, aged face. Before a gentle warming smile formed.

"My Lady, why do you want him?"

"I am requesting you to drop the charges,"

Alessandria looked at him. Her eyes narrowing as the Lord Justice fought to contain his laughter.

"My Lady Fireheart, even if I could release

him, I would not. He is a criminal and a member of the Serpent Gang. Merely because he does not operate on Fireheart land does not mean he should go free,"

Nemesio stepped forward. His eyes narrowing on the Lord Justice.

"You said if you could release him. You are the Lord Justice. You can release everyone unless the Queen overrules you. If that is your concern, we promise you the Queen will not overrule you,"

"Noble friend, I appreciate that, but the Queen is not my concern in this regard, but the Serpentine is dead. Murdered by a man in a black cloak two hours ago. We killed the man on site,"

Nemesio grabbed Alessandria's arm and pulled her aside.

"They must have known we needed him," he whispered.

"No one knew. Daniel and Hellen wouldn't have told anyone,"

"In all fairness, it's a good guess we were being monitored. The mastermind would know we went to see the Serpent Gang. It's probable her grandson is what she would bargain for,"

"Nemesio, what now?"

Nemesio stopped and shook his head.

Alessandria completely agreed. This was the one shot they had at finding the person who hired the assassins. Maybe the fact that these assassins killed her Grandson might shake her tongue loose, but

Alessandria doubted it. Criminals didn't normally work like that. Sure she might find the mastermind's body in a few days, but she wanted to do this right.

"We need to go to Harrison's and regroup. Hopefully, Daniel and Hellen found something," Alessandria explained.

"Agreed,"

A body fell to the floor.

Alessandria turned around.

The Lord Justice laid on the floor unconscious.

Five black cloaked assassins stood around him. Each armed with a crossbow.

This was no fight they could win.

Nemesio didn't seem to care.

He darted forward.

The enemy fired.

Two crossbow bolts hit his armour. Piercing it.

He roared in pain.

The enemy reloaded.

Alessandria grabbed Nemesio.

The Assassins fired.

Alessandria pulled Nemesio away.

A bolt shot into her leg.

Her and Nemesio jumped up.

Nemesio supported Alessandria.

She bit back the pain as she felt the blood dripping from the wound.

An assassin screamed.

Alessandria and Nemesio rapidly hopped along together.

She looked back briefly to see the Lord Justice thrusting a small dagger into the leg of an Assassin.

They kept going.

CHAPTER 14

Closing my eyes briefly to get a moment of calm I felt the cold metal of my dulled blade as I turned it in my left hand. While I leaned into the soft white square cushions of Harrison's sofa that was thankfully warm as I had been sitting here for a few minutes.

Opening my eyes, I looked at the piece of cloth that Harrison had used to put pressure on my wound. Thankfully it was just a flesh wound, a very painful flesh wound I add. Harrison had said and I concurred with him after remembering my Military days. There were a lot of flesh wounds back then!

Turning my attention to Harrison, he laid on the sofa, topless, with his head resting on my leg and I played with his beautifully soft hair. I know it's weird but I always found this calming, and he didn't mind.

Sadly taking my attention away from him, I looked to the other sofa adjacent to our one to see Alessandria and Hellen in their black and grey Procurator cloaks and Nemesio in his forsaken blue and red fiery armour sitting comfortably together. But I couldn't believe that the Inquisitor had his feet on

Harrison's brown oak coffee table. Even worse he was gently humming!

I hate humming or anything that creates extra noise. How dare he? I don't want to keep listening to a barely audible humming. It's so annoying. But I kept playing with Harrison's beautiful hair.

Although I did see Nemesio admiring Harrison's small cottage, you might as well call it, and I too had an appreciative look. Admiring the old drawings on the walls, the stove and the lovely fireplace. As well as the new items that I had bought us when Harrison made me buy some stuff so we could call the place ours. I didn't mind so I bought some small paintings of Military battles and some books on Military history from my room at the castle.

I know normally I would have hated the idea of moving these paintings and books. Yet now I didn't even hesitate. I knew I loved him and I was more than ready to start this new chapter of my... Our life together. Just for the hell of it, I looked down and gave Harrison a quick kiss.

Returning my attention, to our house guest I had to admit considering Nemesio was in his awful armour and he was here. I was a lot calmer than I thought I'll be. Maybe it's because I'm playing with my dulled blade and Harrison's hair. But I like to think it's because I'm getting better.

What concerned me though was Alessandria's story about cloaked men attacking her and Nemesio. Thankfully, Harrison patched her up too and against his better judgement he patched up Nemesio too. He had some old healing potion of a witch he knew once so he gave it to Alessandria. Saying she'll be fine tomorrow. I really hope so. I don't want her to be in pain.

Immediately, I flinched as I saw Nemesio open his mouth and speak: "Thank you, Harrison for patching us up. You have a lovely house,"

Harrison simply nodded and ignored the compliment. We both agreed they were pointless words. Did it matter if he liked *our* house?

"Alessandria, what happened exactly again?" I asked.

Alessandria tapped Nemesio's legs to get him to remove them from the table as she replied: "We were talking to the Lord Justice about the Serpentine boy and these assassins just turned up. They must have been hiding in the office,"

"Strange," I added.

"At least me and Daniel found something. We were artful. Even with those women shooting at us,"

"Thank you, Hellen," Alessandria smiled.

"But this makes no sense," I said. "Let's recap, what do we know?"

"We know earlier today a group of assassins got let into the Queen's official talking thing and tried to kill her. These people were hired by an unknown figure who is only known to the Leader of the Serpent Gang. She bargained the name for the release of her Grandson, who these assassins killed for an unknown purpose," Alessandria explained.

"Meanwhile, Ares, who is most certainly this figure, has been sieging the Greenscales land and trying to raise an army for an unknown crusade. He has even gone as far as to cover his tracks by faking all the necessary legal documents. Even the Queen's signature is fake,"

"What ya mean Unknown Crusade?" Hellen asked.

"He says he wants to invade Mortisical, but I don't believe him. I think he wants to take the palace,"

"But he doesn't need a secret army, does he? He could just use the men under his command," Harrison asked.

Continuing to play with his hair, I replied: "Not necessarily, the majority of the soldiers at the palace and in the military worship the Queen as a divine being. They would never support a coup against her,"

He nodded.

"What about this Triad the assassins referred to?" Nemesio inquired.

"Well, a Triad means three," Alessandria explained. "So, I think there are three masterminds behind these assassination attempts. Sure, Ares' could be one, but who are the others? And we need proof. Ares has too much political power for the Queen to just arrest him without proof. That could put her reign in even more uncertainty,"

Laying out my head to look up at the wooden ceiling, I asked: "What now?"

Raising my head again, I saw Alessandria

stand up and stretch her arms. Whilst Nemesio stared at her. I wanted to smile at his lack of subtlety, but something told me not to.

Walking over to me, Alessandria said: "Well, it's almost eleven o'clock at night and I need to go to bed. Tomorrow I'll go and see the old Lady Serpentine again and hopefully she'll give us the name,"

Alessandria leaned over Harrison, I felt him tense, and she gave me a hug and a kiss on the forehead.

As the three of them walked out the door, Alessandria added: "Harrison, Daniel has something he wants to talk to you about?"

I smiled and shook my head at her. Trust her to make me talk about the topic.

When the wooden door shut, Harrison rolled onto his side. His head still resting on my leg and he smiled at me.

"What you want to talk about?"

"Me and Alessandria were talking earlier, and she said I should just tell you,"

Lifting up his arms, he grabbed his hands and said: "Daniel, if it's about *doing it*. I will wait for as long as you need,"

I allowed a weird laugh to come out.

"No, it's just...I want to. I really, really do. It's my dream. I'm just not sure if I can cope with all the touching and the physical aspects of it. Hell, I collapsed from exhaustion earlier over nothing,"

"Babe, I'm scared too,"

"Why you've done it before?"

"With women, not men. And I get it, we both hate being touched by others and we hate noise and everything else that can annoy us. So, when you're ready, we'll just take it slow and see how it goes. Daniel, I love you so relax,"

I gave him another quick kiss.

Then Harrison replied: "We aren't trying it tonight. I'm too tired,"

Then he simply walked away.

CHAPTER 15

Looking out over all the little stone buildings and thatch houses of the city and columns of smoke rising out of the majority of them. Alessandria sat out on the little balcony, with its waist-high stone pillars and guard rail and little marble squares acting as the floor, enjoying the sight of the city. Whilst the morning sun shone blood red as it continued to rise.

As she focused on the beauty of the clouds turned blood red by the sunlight, her hands stretched over to the small white table next to her filled with a few sweet Iced pastries and slices of toast.

Turning to look at the table, Alessandria picked up a small silver table knife and spread some butter on her toast. The sound of the knife scratching the bread almost echoing on the smooth castle walls behind her.

The sound of a dropped knife hitting a fine china plate reminded Alessandria of Hellen's presence. She wasn't sure who's idea it was to have such a posh and noble breakfast together on a castle balcony but they needed to do it more often.

Alessandria thought as the buttery taste of the toast filled her mouth.

Looking at Hellen, Alessandria considered what she usually ate for breakfast. Scraps? Despite being good friends for at least two years, they never had met much before ten in the morning. Alessandria thought that was down to Hellen's busy male schedule, but who knows?

Whatever the answer Alessandria needed to make sure this happened again. For it had been a great two hours of talking, catching up and just being friends whilst they waited for Nemesio to return from the Serpent gang.

Of course, she had thought the old lady requesting his presence at the break of dawn was odd but she only knew this because Nemesio had left her a note. At least she got a bit of free time to just be a friend.

Although, as far as the note Nemesio left was concerned, Alessandria was far more interested in the fact that Nemesio had made it clear he didn't want to disturb her sleep. Did he really care about her that much? He was a former Inquisitor, he was used to disturbing people. He used to do it for a living. Was this him changing or did he care about her?

The delicious smell of sweet fruity buttery pastries made Alessandria return from her thinking as she saw Hellen feast on a few pastries. Smiling as she did so.

"Enjoying the breakfast," Alessandria asked.

"Yea, this is great. Is this how the nobility normally eats?"

"Most days, yes,"

Hellen nodded her approval as she ate another pastry.

"How comes we've never had breakfast together before?" Alessandria asked.

"I don't know but I want to. Especially, if ya serve food like this!"

"What do you normally eat?"

Hellen was about to speak before she closed her mouth to finish chewing a piece of chunky strawberry jam.

"Normally, I eat toast or leftovers from the night before,"

Alessandria nodded, wishing that her friend ate better.

"So, Nemesio was staring at ya last night,"

The Dominicus Procurator smiled and rolled her eyes.

"Not you too. Daniel asked me if I found Nemesio attractive,"

"Well, he is. He's strong and now he's left the Order. He's a good guy in great shape,"

Alessandria gave a small nod as she thought about it. She wasn't wrong he was attractive, but how well did she know him? She had only known him three, coming up four weeks. Was that too soon to like someone?

"I agree but we're just work friends,"

"He likes ya. I know it,"

Alessandria's blushed a little.

"Come on, he has a great body. What did

33

Daniel think of it?"

"He didn't common on Nemesio's looks but he gave me his blessing if I liked Nemesio,"

"What more do ya need?"

Opening her mouth to speak, the words died out in Alessandria's throat as she couldn't think of a counter-argument. Hellen was right of course. She didn't need anything. She had her brother's blessing, the most important thing, and she liked Nemesio, the second most important thing to her. What was she waiting for?

"I'll think about it, I promise,"

"That's my girl," Hellen replied as she ate another triangle of buttered toast.

To the left of Alessandria, the wooden door opened and Nemesio in his strong muscular blue and red fiery armour walked towards them. He crouched next to Alessandria with there not being a free chair.

Feeling his body heat, Alessandria began to feel warm and awkward. Maybe she should talk to him or even ask him out. No, that wasn't appropriate. The Nobility wouldn't allow that to stand, a woman asking out a man. Ridiculous!

However, Alessandria started to think about her family's bad standing because of Daniel. Would it matter if her family broke another tradition?

"What's ya thinking about?" Hellen teased.

"Um, nothing," Alessandria replied as she turned to look at Nemesio. "What did the Lady Serpentine want?"

Nemesio made an interesting smile as he picked up a triangle pastry.

"It turns out, the Serpentine is actually a Noble Family. A few kings ago, there was a deal between the King and her great grandfather. They rule the underworld under a few conditions,"

"Do they have a seat in the court?"

"Yes and the Lady Serpentine confirmed they have a lot of influence over the House of Gravers,"

"So getting their supports gets me the Gravers too?"

"Correct,"

Alessandria nodded as she thought about the Church, the House of Blueheart and the other Inquisitorial Orders that she needed to get. There were still so many voices she didn't have. That would change in time, regardless of who objected. At least that was the plan.

"But why did she request your presence?" Alessandria asked.

Standing up and stretching his legs, Nemesio explained.

"She was furious that Danic was murdered so she pledged her support to you, and she gave me the name,"

Standing up, Alessandria asked very firmly: "Who?"

"Lord Commander Ares,"

CHAPTER 16

As I looked up and down the immense stone corridor waiting for Alessandria and Nemesio, I was thrilled that we were finally going to take down this corrupt official.

Of course, I had wanted to storm into the office without them and take him down. But Alessandria's note was very firm that I needed to wait for her. She's so boring sometimes!

Anyway, I was stuck waiting for them. Just standing in the shadows of a stone staircase. Looking at the boring grey stone walls and ceiling while I waited.

Well, at least I had some impressive paintings from centuries ago to look at. The painting directly in front of me was of the harbour filled with hundreds of ships unloading spices, sugar and other extremely precious cargo. I shook my head and spun my dulled blade slowly as I remembered Ordericous hadn't had a day like that for centuries. The war with Mortisical hadn't helped nor the other decisions of past kings.

Perhaps I might try and change that in the future, I don't know how but it would be good for the people. Then I almost laughed at myself for starting to think as a leader.

Maybe Alessandria was on to something. Maybe I could lead a Noble House successfully. Even now I wanted to rid this country of a traitor so perhaps I could lead and serve the Queen. But I know my sister has a long way to go yet with her family.

Looking around again, there was still no sign of them. I hate people being late! Well, they weren't late but they were taking their time to get here.

Poking my head further out of the shadows of the staircase, I looked towards the far end of the corridor where Ares' office was. So badly I wanted to charge in there, attack him and end his treachery, but spun my dulled blade faster and decided to wait.

Although, I got the odd smell of oranges and sweet honey for an unknown reason. Maybe he was burning incense in his office?

Getting almost bored of waiting, I took a few steps out into the corridor, feeling the cool morning breeze blow past me and the soft red carpet under my feet.

Finally, I heard the typical sound of Hellen's big stick tapping on the stone floor. Turning around I saw them walk towards me. My dulled blade turned faster at the sight of Nemesio in his blue and fiery red armour, but I remained calm.

Looking at Hellen, she gave me a cheerful smile. She too was probably excited by the idea of getting to thump someone over the head. Then Alessandria nodded in my direction wearing her usual black leather armour. But she smelt of pastries and honey. Could that be what I smelt earlier?

When they reached me, they kept walking. I

joined them. Together as one force, we walked towards the wooden door to Ares office.

Once we reached it, Alessandria nodded to Hellen.

She charged forward.

Whacking the door with her big stick.

Amazingly, it broke open.

We charged it.

I whipped out my sword.

My eyes searched for Ares.

Nothing.

I only saw the same boring stone walls and tiny desk as earlier.

Hellen smashed her stick down in frustration.

My dulled blade turned faster in frustration.

I wanted to lash out at him.

However, taking a deep breath, I calmed myself. He wasn't here that was out of my control. No point getting annoyed about the little things. I'll leave that to the non-autistic people.

Looking at Alessandria and Nemesio, they shook their heads in frustration and Nemesio went over to stand by the door. Presumably, in case Ares walked up the corridor.

"The room's clear," Alessandria said as she passed me the Arrest Warrant signed by the Queen herself and the Lord Justice.

I'm not particularly sure why the Lord Justice needed to sign it, but I couldn't care less about Procurator politics.

"He has not been here for a while," I added as I pointed to the furry sandwich on his desk.

We both turned towards the desk as Hellen tripped over some of the empty drink bottles.

"Daniel, do you think mother's okay?"

"She will be fine. She's in a locked complex with hundreds of people to talk to and scheme for and against. Do you really think she isn't having the time of her life?"

"Good point," she laughed.

"She'll be fine, Alessandria. My concern is where is Ares? He should be here. He wouldn't have known Lady Serpentine gave him up,"

"A matter of time perhaps until she did?"

"Killing her Grandchild was a poor move. The better idea would be to kidnap him and force her not to tell us,"

"You've given this some thought,"

"If my military history obsession has taught me anything. It's you need to spend as much time thinking like the enemy than a loyal soldier,"

Alessandria simply nodded.

"If I was Ares, I would've… I don't know. He has nowhere to go,"

"Exactly, dear sister. He has nothing left to lose,"

"Suicide?"

I smiled at the comment.

"As a person who almost did, this isn't enough to drive him to it. And all his behaviour seems to be driven by the death of the Queen. And he still has the support of the Triad presumably, so suicide is too doubtful,"

"What ya make of these?" Hellen asked as she pointed to piles of parchment on the desk.

I rushed over and waved Alessandria over.

She flicked through the pages of parchment with thick layers of text and diagrams. The cold parchment felt strange in my hands, as did the ancient smell of the parchment. Almost as if it were mouldy.

"These are diagrams of the bridge near the main river a few kilometres away," Alessandria explained.

"I have some schematics about carriages. The weak points are highlighted," Hellen added.

I took those schematics and said: "I'll show them to Harrison to see if they're important,"

Alessandria asked: "Would you be okay in the engineering room? It's loud and sweaty,"

"I'll have to be for the Queen,"

Alessandria nodded.

Placing my pieces of parchment on the desk, I said: "And these drawings and recipes of gunpowder,"

"Wait, Alessandria didn't ya say the Queen gonna to the Outer most military Base in Ordericous today?"

"She would have to cross that bridge," I added.

"They're going to blow up on the bridge

when she crosses it," Alessandria finished. Dashing out the room to avert disaster.

CHAPTER 17

As their horses thumped along the hard dirt road, Alessandria, Hellen and Nemesio braced themselves as their horses stomped their hooves into the road. Travelling as fast as they could.

As the horses galloped along, Alessandria felt the air whipped past her and her long strong hair whipped wildly in the wind. She wanted it to stop but her hair refused. Continuing to go wild and occasionally cover her face.

Thankfully, these were Fireheart horses, immensely muscular black and brown horses bred for war. Despite these horses looking harmless, Alessandria knew these would easily kill a man and it could run much faster than a normal horse. And that is what she needed.

Breathing in the fresh countryside air, Alessandria saw the massive knobby trees with their large spiky leaves turn to blurs as the horses picked up their pace.

They needed to get to the bridge before the Queen. Alessandria's stomach began to flip at the thought of the Queen dying in the explosion of the bridge.

She was not going to let that happen, not to her Queen.

Shaking the reins of the horse, Alessandria willed it to go faster but they were already travelling so fast Alessandria couldn't see Nemesio and Hellen properly. They were mere blurry shapes next to her.

With the wind continuing to whip past her creating an immense howl in her ears, Alessandria raised her head and smiled as she roughly saw the bridge. Thankfully, as she was travelling towards it, she could see it.

In all of its stone might as the grey arched Bridge looked as if it had grown out of the ground and stretched to the other side.

Alessandria searched for the Queen on their side of the bridge. She found them.

About twenty metres from the bridge, there was a large black and red carriage rolling along with twenty armoured guards on horseback riding next to her.

Delight filled Alessandria for finding her Queen before it was too late, but the Queen was still heading towards the bridge.

They kept riding.

Pointlessly, Alessandria started to wave her hands about. Hoping that a guard would see her. She even laughed at herself after a few moments.

The horses started to slow down.

They were growing tired.

Alessandria's eyes widened as the horses continued to slow. This wasn't happening.

Alessandria was not going to let her Queen die.

She pulled the reins hard.

The horse stopped.

Alessandria jumped off and started running. Cutting across the thick green grassland to reach her Queen.

She screamed.

She shouted.

She waved her arms in a crazy pattern.

Nemesio and Hellen kept riding, but their horses were slowing.

Then it hit her.

Alessandria pulled out a small one-shot pistol her father had given her.

She ran.

Aiming up the Queen's carriage.

The Queen was almost at the bridge.

Alessandria aimed and fired.

A Guard was knocked off his horse.

The Guards turned around on their horses.

Nemesio grabbed Alessandria and rode to the Guards.

The Guards must have seen Nemesio's armour and decided not to shoot.

The Queen kept riding towards the bridge.

When she was within shouting distance, Alessandria screamed: "Stop the carriage! There's a bomb,"

Immediately, all the Guards whipped out their small horns and gave them a long deep blow.

A deafening howl echoed around the land.

Alessandria's eyes lit up as the carriage stopped ten metres from the stone bridge.

She jumped off the horse and ran to the carriage.

Opening it, she found it empty. Her heart sank and a wave of confusion washed over her.

A horse slowly walked over to her. Looking up, Alessandria saw a woman in the thick white armour plating of a Guard.

"Looking for me?" the Queen said as she stepped off the horse.

"You always were clever,"

"Not clever enough this time. A bomb still would have killed me,"

"Agreed but…"

An explosion drowned out Alessandria's words.

Immense chunks of flaming stone rained down upon them.

Horses screamed as they were smashed to pieces.

The Guards shrieked as they were burnt alive.

Alessandria jumped on the Queen.

Another bomb.

The Carriage exploded.

A veil of smoke filled Alessandria's vision.

She moved away clearing it.

More guards screamed as their throats were split.

Five black cloaked men advanced from the river.

The air stunk of gunpowder and burnt flesh.

More Guards were slaughtered in seconds.

Alessandria stood in front of the Queen as three men stood there.

They charged.

Alessandria whipped out her sword but it was too late.

The men knocked her aside.

Alessandria whacked her head on the stone chunks of the bridge.

The searing heat adding to her pain.

A cut and burn ran along her forehead.

She tried to stand up. She couldn't.

She looked at the Queen.

The Queen whipped out two long shining swords. She swung them.

The men tried to block.

The Queen's swords went straight through the assassins' swords.

The broken shards of metal glowed white before they turned to dust.

Her swords glowed red in return.

They took a step back.

A scream followed by the sound of Hellen's stick comforted Alessandria.

Another scream followed by the sound of a skull-cracking made Alessandria smile.

She stood up.

Marched over to the three men and slash at the chest of one of them.

His blood sprayed over Alessandria's armour. Warming it slightly.

Another man went for the Queen.

Hellen appeared from behind.

Bringing her stick down on the man's head.

The last man started laughing.

"Ares did not tell us you were powerful. He lied. The idiot. It matters not," he turned to Alessandria. "Your freak of a brother will die next,"

Alessandria was about to grab him when the man darted for the Queen with the rest of his sword. Forcing the Queen to kill him.

A great fear built up in Alessandria as the thought of Daniel's dead body entered her mind. She couldn't lose him not after growing close to him again.

CHAPTER 18

As I stepped into the engineering chamber, I had to spin my dulled blade quicker and quicker to remain calm as I heard the deafening banging of hammering, the roaring of fires and shouting of men. This was a nightmare. I hated loud noises. I hated them but I reminded myself that I was here for my Queen and seeing Harrison working wouldn't be all bad.

Forcing myself forward, I walked past tens of red and black carriages with men pounding hammers against them. Presumably, hammering in New wheels or whatever these people do.

I know Harrison talks about his work when we get home but I sometimes zone out pretending to be interested with the timely nod or sound of agreement. Mother once said with those abilities I was cut out for marriage. I'll think about that in the far future.

Continuing to pass the rows upon rows of carriages and men walking in and out of the rows carrying heavy leather bags filled with tools. I flinched and gasped at the sound of every hammer. It was ridiculous!

The smell of oil and burning coal filled my senses. It was awful. How could people work like this every day?

Taking a deep breath, I focused on the feeling of the cold metal of my dulled blade and the look at the rough stone beneath my leather booted feet and I started walking again.

Luckily, I knew where Harrison's great station was, in the middle of the chamber. Meaning I had to pass tens of hammering men and women and tens upon tens of damaged carriages.

As I kept walking, I realised why I hadn't come to see Harrison on his lunch break or even met him here after his shift. I despised this place. The noise, the noise, the noise it was too much.

My dulled blade span as fast as it could. With each hammering of the metal and carriages, I could feel my body getting more and more shaky and hunched. I wanted to go.

A grand hiss of steam on the far side of the chamber made me jump.

Memories of the torture sessions filled my mind.

Images of the red hot pokers appeared.

More hammering continued.

More noise.

More shouting.

My senses couldn't take it.

I fell to the floor, crawled up in a ball and cried loudly.

I closed my eyes. Feeling the tears streaming down my face. As much as I loved my autism for the benefits it has, I hated the sensitivity to noise. Why couldn't the engineers stop? Please.

I just wanted them to stop.

As I continued to shake and cry my eyes out, I heard a set of footsteps come up to me and shout: "Boss, your man's here! "

Why did he have to shout?

The set of footsteps quickly left, and another wandered up to me. I heard the figure knelt down next to me.

"Daniel?" I heard Harrison's voice asked.

Raising my head, tears continued to stream down my face, and I fell in Harrison's arms. He gently rubbed my back.

"What's wrong?"

"The noise," I forced out through crying teeth.

Covering my ears with his rough yet loving hands, he screamed: "Everyone take twenty. That's an order,"

No one complained and quickly everyone left.

"Daniel, you're safe," he said as my crying started to stop. "Why are you even down here? You never visit me at work,"

Of course, it dawned on me then that Harrison was at work and the warm skin that warmed my sobering face was his chest.

Forcing myself to come together, I looked at his soft blue eyes and answered his question.

"Ares, he is a traitor and he found these on his desk," I replied as I took out the parchment depicting the carriages out from my leather trench coat.

Harrison opened it and unwrapped his arm around me to read it.

"We believe the circles are weak points that the assassins are trying to target,"

Harrison kept trying.

"Are we correct?"

Harrison folded up the parchment and gave it back to me. I put it back in my pocket. Then he smiled.

"Daniel, they're just circles. They're meaningless,"

I stood up and faced him.

Standing up he said, "Daniel, were you always going to come here to check these with me?"

I'm not sure if I understood the question but I nodded.

"If I was Ares, I would make sure I left some plans that would make someone come to the engineering department,"

"Your point?"

Instead of talking, Harrison grabbed my arm and we started to walk away. He walked up along two rows of red and black carriages.

"I think it's a trap. I didn't think too much but the door was unlocked when I came in. I always lock it before I leave at night,"

As soon as the words left his beautiful mouth, ten black cloaked men and women stepped out from behind the carriages. They got out their swords.

No crossbows.

I placed my arm protectively in front of Harrison.

"Your Queen is dead. Your Kingdom will fall. Ares will rise to power," one of the cloaked men said.

"I may not know who you are, but I know your friends have died by my hands. And the same will happen to you!" I said.

I charged.

Whipping out my blade.

I swung my sword.

The enemy dived out the way.

They jumped at me.

I dodged their sword swings.

Their swords hacked into the wooden carriages.

Harrison grabbed a metal crowbar.

He threw it.

Cracking the skull of one man.

Blood sprayed into the air. Raining down upon us.

He gasped.

An assassin charged at Harrison.

I tackled him.

Smashing my fist into his head.

The sound of rushing air made me jump to one side.

A sword fell. Killing the assassin I punched.

The sword falling assassin I slashed his throat.

I grabbed Harrison.

Pulling him further into the engineering chamber.

The assassins raced after us. Swords swinging.

CHAPTER 19

Walking down the awful boring stone corridor towards the engineering chamber, Alessandria's heart thumped inside her chest. She couldn't believe the enemy were trying something against her brother.

The sound of Hellen's stick tapping against the stone floor echoed around the corridor as they walked. Nemesio had tried to comfort her on the way to the castle but she wasn't having any of it. Her brother was in danger.

She could almost smell the fearful sweat on her as she walked towards the chamber.

Alessandria felt the cold sweat drip down her back.

Seeing the door at the end of the stone corridor, a strange sense of rage built within Alessandria. She wanted to bust in there and kill all these assassins. No one attacks her family and gets to live.

However, the Procurator part of her wanted Alessandria to subdue them and arrest them. That was the proper and right way. Yet she didn't care this was her brother!

Hellen dashed past her and tried to open the door. She couldn't.

Alessandria slowed to a gentle stroll at the thought of not being able to get to Daniel. He probably had enough trouble in the engineering room.

She passed an engineer in a large crowd who mentioned Harrison had ordered them to take a break after finding Daniel. Well, the engineer called Daniel a worse name than freak. So she broke the man's nose.

This only made her want to pound down that door. Her brother needed her.

The Queen walked past her and placed her hand on top of Alessandria's and gave her hand a caring rub. Giving Alessandria the distinct flowery smell of the Queen's perfume.

Looking back at the door, Alessandria rushed over as she saw Nemesio back away and Hellen used her big stick as a crowbar and forced the door open.

With a loud bang, they were in.

They all stormed in.

Charging in, Alessandria saw the rows upon rows of red and black carriages.

The air smelt of fear and vapourised blood.

A scream caught her attention.

It was Harrison.

Alessandria started to run down the rows of carriages to find her brother.

The others follow.

Alessandria hated the rows of carriages.

An assassin tackled Alessandria as she ran.

Her head hit the wheel of a carriage.

Hellen whacked the assassin's head with her stick.

Alessandria jumped up. She continued running.

Another assassin jumped down from the top of a carriage.

The Queen surged forward.

Slicing through the assassin's thick armour with her glowing swords.

Another scream.

A loud bang echoed all around Alessandria.

They needed to hurry.

They kept running down a long row of red and black carriages.

A small boom made a carriage fall in front of Alessandria.

It busted into flames.

The Queen roared in frustration.

Alessandria squeezed through a gap to another row of carriages.

The others followed.

A sword flashed before her eyes.

It came towards her.

Alessandria reflexed up her forearm.

The sword smashed into her leather armour.

Tearing it.

Alessandria jumped out of the gap. Punching the Assassin in the face.

Giving her precious seconds to snap the neck of the assassin.

She pressed on.

She needed to find Daniel.

She charged down the row of carriages.

More carriages exploded behind her.

She wanted to check on her friends, but she needed to find Daniel.

The sound of Hellen's stick whacking flesh alerted her to more assassins.

A drop of sweat ran down her spine.

She kept running.

She came to the end of the row.

Coming out at a massive stone circle. Surrounded by damaged carriages.

She saw Daniel fighting with an assassin.

There were ten of them surrounding Daniel and Harrison.

Rage built inside her.

Alessandria screamed in rage.

Three assassins came to her.

She charged.

Swinging her sword wildly.

One assassin tried to block it.

The sheer force of Alessandria's swing broke his hand.

She grabbed his throat. Her nails ripping into his flesh.

The other two assassins swung at her.

Alessandria released the assassin and dived out the way.

The assassin gasped in pain.

Nemesio ran behind Alessandria. Firing his pistol. Killing the two assassins.

Alessandria smashed her foot into the face of the gasping assassin.

Bones shattered.

His corpse thumped onto the stone floor.

Alessandria looked at Daniel and Harrison.

Four corpses laid dead at their feet.

There was one more assassin. She swung at Harrison.

Alessandria and Nemesio charged.

Daniel surged forward. Sinking his long nails into her flesh.

Her blood squirted out.

Harrison thrusted a sword into her chest. Killing her.

It was over.

Catching her breath, Alessandria ran over to Daniel and hugged him. He tensed but she didn't care. He was safe and alive. Then she hugged Harrison and took a few steps back.

Looking behind her, Alessandria beamed as she saw the Queen, Hellen and Nemesio walk towards her smiling. They must have enjoyed the killing and Alessandria couldn't blame them. They had made Ares fail.

Whilst, Alessandria still might have been confused to why Ares had ordered the last of his assassins to target Daniel and Harrison. She was glad he failed.

As she looked at her brother, she knew she cared about him and she knew she was never ever going to let anything bad happen to him. A part of her wanted to talk to Harrison to make sure he never hurt her brother but this wasn't the time not the place.

"Ya missed some great killing. That Queen and I, we slain some baddies,"

Both Daniel and Harrison looked confused at each other.

"What's wrong?" Alessandria asked.

"There were only ten assassins. We killed some and fled to here. Who were you fighting?"

Alessandria looked widen eyed at Nemesio and Hellen.

"Daniel, we were fighting assassins,"

The Queen grabbed Hellen and pulled her into the large stone circle where Daniel and Harrison stood. Alessandria and Nemesio joined her with their swords out.

"This is a trap," she stated.

More carriages exploded.

Flaming shards of wood rained down.

The doors of the remaining carriages opened. Out walked tens upon tens of assassins.

They whipped out their curved swords. Dripping with bright green poison.

Slowly walking towards Alessandria and her friends.

CHAPTER 20

Turning my dulled blade in my hand, I knew this was ridiculous!

As Alessandria, Nemesio, Hellen and the Queen joined me and Harrison in forming a defensive line in the middle of the massive grey stone circle we stood on. I realised I really didn't care for this.

I wasn't stressed or anything as I breathed in the smoke from the burning carriages around the edges of the chamber. I was just annoyed by this all as the tens of assassins in black cloaks slowly walked towards us.

Whilst I had to admit they were clever in their design and plan. They knew they had us trapped and now we had to make a final stand, so they continued to slowly walk towards us with their swords sharp. I knew I wasn't meant to die today.

Partly because I believed too much in Alessandria, she would have her support and I would be made Lord Fireheart and so would Harrison in a way. And after my beautiful, wonderful sister came to save me. I was not going to let her down.

For the first time in weeks, since I found Harrison again, a wave of emotion waved over me. Having emotion always felt strange but I was determined to live.

Narrowing my eyes, I focused. I needed to find a way out of here.

Looking around, all I saw the burning remains of red and black carriages lining the edges of the chamber and the outside of this ring. The massive bright yellow flames danced in the fire. Devouring the wood and paint. Sending thin columns of smoke into the air.

Raising my head, I looked at the blackening domed ceiling and thankfully the top of the ceiling was glass. For some reason it was cracked, allowing the smoke to escape. I didn't care how it cracked and broke, only that it was.

As I focused on the abominable black cloaked assassins, I felt the disgusting taste of soot and ash in my mouth, as well as a thin coating of ash-covered my skin. The assassins all looked the same in their black cloaks with their two long silver swords.

However, the most unnerving thing was all the assassins walked as one. As one took a step, they all took a step.

I knew we were going to die.

If I could have any wish right now, it would be to save my friends and Harrison. I know I hate people with a passion but I love these people. I love my sister, Hellen, the Queen and Harrison. And if Alessandria likes Nemesio then I needed to save him too.

Looking at each of them individually, I made sure if I was going to die then I would remember

Hellen in her dirty grey cloak and her big stick. The Queen in her stunning white armour. Nemesio in that awful blue and red fiery armour that I hate. My beautiful sister and her furious desire to protect her family.

Then Harrison, the man I loved and the man I put through so much pain and lost so much time with.

Turning my attention back to the assassins, they were close now. Maybe just twenty metres away. I knew what I had to do but I was scared of the consequences. But at least I fixed my friends into my memory.

My dulled blade spun fast in my hand before I made myself put it away and I grabbed Harrison's hand, I looked at Alessandria and said:

"Alessandria, let me break the bottle,"

As soon as the word reached her ears, I could see the conflict in her eyes. I knew she hated the idea, but we were outnumbered. We were all going to die.

"I feel different this time. I can control it,"

Whispering, Alessandria replied: "Break the bottle,"

Everyone got behind.

Harrison kissed me before he went.

I stared at the mortal fools.

How dare they attack us!

These are my friends, and I will defend them.

Letting my hate and rage take over, I could feel my tension release and my long nails hardened into claws.

My eyes turned black.

All I wanted was to kill.

I charged.

The assassins swung their swords.

They hit me.

They didn't cut me.

I sunk my claws into the warm flesh of the assassins.

They screamed.

I laughed as their blood painted the floor.

My teeth ripped into their warm flesh.

I dashed over to another group of assassins.

Slashing their chests with my claws before drinking their blood.

Three assassins charged towards Alessandria.

I stormed out. Ripping out the assassins' spines.

A group of assassins charged at me.

I kicked them all hard.

The sound of shattering bones filled the air.

More assassins screamed as my claws sunk into them.

Their horrific memories filled my mind.

I did not care.

I only laughed at their mortal existence.

More assassins threw daggers at my back.

The daggers bounced off.

I turned.

The assassins snarled.

I snarled louder.

I rushed over to them. Painting the stone

circle with their flesh, organs, and blood.

Three assassins left.

They whipped out their pistols.

Firing them at the Queen.

I could see the bullets.

Dashing over, I caught the red-hot bullets.

I didn't care about the heat. I was in control of the Flesheater ability.

The assassins froze.

It was over.

Snarling at them as I walked, I raised my claws and beheaded them all.

Their heads landed with a thump. Leaving a trail of dark red rich blood on the stone floor.

All the assassins were dead.

With shaking hands, I took out my dulled blade and played with it. Focusing on my mind, regaining my control. I felt Harrison's warm body next to mine. His hand gently holding my other blood-soaked claw.

After embracing Harrison's touch and the humanity of it, and a few deep breaths. My claws became normal nails again and my eyes returned to normal.

Immediately, I hugged Harrison and looked to Alessandria over his shoulder. She smiled and nodded her thanks to me.

CHAPTER 21

Walking slowly towards the heavy black cast iron door at the end of the stone corridor, Alessandria couldn't wait to open it and end Ares. His death sentence was long overdue.

After Daniel's use of the Flesheater ability and their subsequent escape, it hadn't taken Alessandria and the Queen long to find Ares. Leading them to the top of the castle where he had reportedly been for a few hours.

Whilst Alessandria didn't understand why he didn't just flee so he could live for a few more days until the Inquisition caught up with him. She was more than glad this was going to be over. At least with Ares.

As she walked towards the door, she noticed the hand painted murals either side of her on the stone walls. They were stunning depictions of the forests to the left and the chaos of War to her right.

Right now, she wanted war. After almost getting her friends and her brother killed. She wanted to Slaughter Ares.

Of course, Alessandria was a Procurator by nature and the fact she was a Dominicus Procurator made her feel guilty about wanting to kill Ares without a trial. Alessandria almost felt as if she was letting her Procurators down and not leading by example.

However, the sound of a big wooden stick tapping on the stone floor made her turn around and walk backwards smiling for a few moments before turning back around. Reminding her this wasn't about being a Procurator, this was being a best friend, a sister and a loyal servant to her Queen. She needed to kill Ares for them, to protect them.

Knowing that Daniel, Hellen and Nemesio were all behind her in this, she turned the door latchet, feeling the cold metal against her skin, and opened the door.

Revealing a massive rooftop balcony with a shiny white marble floor and beautifully carved marble pillars with a golden guard railing running along the top of the pillars.

Stepping out onto the balcony, the warm afternoon sun gently warmed her skin and the sun shone dimly reflecting on the shiny marble.

Continuing to walk out onto the balcony, the warm salty air filled her nose, making her want to sneeze. Then she saw him. Alessandria saw Ares leaning against the guard rail staring out over the country he had just tried to destroy.

Looking back at Daniel and her friends, they all nodded. They all wanted her to have the honour and she was not going to resist.

"Ares!" Alessandria shouted as she walked to

8

him and stopped a few metres from him.

"I really tried you know. I wanted to be successful. I wanted to rule,"

"That was never your choice, and you were successful. You were loved and admired by the men and women that served under you,"

"Perhaps, but I wanted to make Ordericous what it once was. We used to be a superpower. If we demanded something other countries would come calling. Then past kings made stupid errors. The military should rule!"

"That is not you to decide. I doubt Ordericous would be better off with a military dictatorship,"

"You don't know that. I would have... ruled and done right by my people,"

"Ha. How? By forcing them into military service and shipping them away to fight your futile wars?"

He nodded.

"It is honourable to serve the throne,"

"Yes, but it is not for everyone,"

"Then those people must die,"

"You have deluded yourself Ares,"

As he started to nod to himself, Alessandria knew that at least a part of him knew what he did was wrong. It was never up to him or any other to decide who sits upon the throne.

However, Alessandria knew she still needed to punish him despite his partial repentance.

"The assassins, why?" she asked.

"I had the money. They're all dead now. Such a waste of money and life. I am sorry for wasting those lives,"

"That is not the point. If there is a god on the other side, then plea with him or her. Do not plea to me,"

Alessandria started to walk slowly towards him. Feeling the cold stone ground as she moved.

"Who is the Triad? You and two others. Who are they?"

"No one you can touch. I might have waited but the Word Bearer will deal with your brother soon enough,"

Alessandria fought her rage back.

"I will not tell you their names. The Word Bearer made sure I wouldn't,"

"Who is the Word Bearer!"

Manically, Ares started laughing.

"This is pointless, Lady Alessandria. I am done. I am finished. You can kill one of the Triad. Be proud. Have a drink. Celebrate but The Firesword will take care of your Queen. There is nothing you can do. It is prophecy the Seer told us so,"

Alessandria noticed Ares was focusing on the drop off the balcony.

She raced to him.

He heard her coming.

He jumped onto the guard rail.

He looked up at her and jumped.

A loud crack echoed around the castle.

Alessandria slowly walked to the guard rail along with her friends and Daniel. She gasped as she saw Ares' body impaled on a large spire on top of one of the towers.

His blood dripped from his lifeless corpse and slowly his body slid further down the spire until it spilt in two.

Turning away from the bloody sight, Alessandria saw everyone with various expressions of horror. Except the Queen only smiled.

CHAPTER 22

Staring at the old drawings on the wall and my Military paintings, I had to admire the beauty of life. We had all defeated a traitor and a threat against the Queen. If that isn't a good day's work then I'm not sure what is.

Of course, I'll experience a bit of annoyance at the change of Military leader. Since I'll have to deal with them on a daily basis. I hope they're competent. I hate useless people.

I immediately smiled as I felt Harrison wrap his arms around me from behind. Feeling his warm breath on my neck.

Turning around, Harrison led me back to the sofa where Alessandria, Nemesio and Hellen were sitting. At least Nemesio didn't have his dirty feet on Harrison's brown oak coffee table.

However, I noticed Nemesio wearing a large brown leather cloak. Covering up his armour for me. A part of me stopped for a moment in confusion. Has he really changed? Was Alessandria truly right?

Then Harrison pulled my arm and I sat down on the sofa. Feeling the sofa square cushions mould to my body and the gentle fabric smooth as I ran my fingers over it.

Looking over at Hellen, I saw her eyeing up her big stick. Checking it for dents and when she found one, she gave a triumphant nod. I suppose we were all happy that everything was over. Ares was dead and the Queen was safe until the other two members of the Triad tried again.

But until then, I was perfectly happy where I was. In the home of my love and with my sister and two friends. Yes, I'm even calling Nemesio a friend now!

As Harrison wrapped his arm around me and leaned slightly against me on the sofa. I got a whiff of his earthy manly aftershave and I thought about how lucky I was, and what Harrison had said earlier about that being the first person he had killed. He had seemed fine and I remember my first kill in the Military, I wasn't upset but it was troubling for a few days. I knew I needed to keep an eye on him.

With my free hand, the other one was wrapped around Harrison, I held my dulled blade. A part of me wanted to spin it but holding it was enough. For I knew I wasn't in any danger here not with my friends.

"Thank ya for the wine," Hellen said as she downed the last of it straight from the large glass bottle in her hand. She placed it on the coffee table when she was done.

"You're welcome," I replied.

"Brother, you don't drink. Neither does Harrison. Why do you have wine?"

"Because dear sister, you never know when

we might have company and we need to celebrate,"

Alessandria nodded but I knew she wasn't convinced.

"Alessandria, we all did a great thing today,"

"But Daniel the two other masterminds still live. You and the Queen aren't safe yet,"

Squeezing Harrison briefly, I replied: "As soon as I knew I was gay. I knew I wouldn't be completely safe. We need to live whilst we can,"

Alessandria shook her head but nodded in the end.

"Daniel, what about the Greenscales?" Hellen asked.

"Yes," I said as she reminded me, and I looked at Alessandria. "I received a letter from her thanking us for the withdrawn of the military from her land. And as promised, she has promised you her family's support on her honour,"

When I saw Alessandria's face light up, I was happy for her. My sister slowly getting her way.

"Thank you, Daniel for arranging that. I promise you I will find the other two members of the Triad before they can hurt you,"

Nemesio tapped her leg carefully and said: "No you won't. We will all find them together,"

Everyone nodded in agreement.

With everything wrapped and Harrison being close to me, I decided to say to everyone: "It is early evening, you could all go out,"

Alessandria looked as if she was about to tell

me off for being rude. Then her face changed to a gentle smile and she blew me a kiss.

"Um, yes. I think I have some paperwork to do at the castle," Alessandria said as she got up. Hellen and Nemesio both clearly understood what I wanted so they got up to leave too

"Nemesio!" I shouted before he left. "I'm sorry. I forgive you, my friend,"

The former Inquisitor looked a bit taken by my comments, but he gave me a sort of confused nod before he left.

As soon as they all left, I turned to Harrison and said: "I'm ready,"

***

Stepping out and shutting the wooden door to Harrison's house, Alessandria took a moment to compose herself. Looking around, she enjoyed seeing the dirt road lined with small stone walls in front of Harrison's little garden. With the trees blowing in the evening wind.

The smell of fresh green grass covered her senses as the evening wind from the coast a few miles away blew gently past her.

Waving goodbye to Hellen, Alessandria couldn't stop smiling as she saw her best friend walk off humming a merry little tune to herself. Tapping the floor with her big stick as she walked.

Raising her head for an unknown reason, Alessandria admired the clear blue evening sky as the dimmish sun reminded her there were plenty of hours of daylight left on this warm summer evening.

She knew this task was done. With the help of her friends and brother, she had killed a threat to her Queen and saved her country. As much as she wanted to enjoy that fact, Alessandria still shook at the idea of two powerful people alive and plotting against Daniel and her Queen.

Nemesio stopped and stood next to her. Joining her in looking at the beautiful countryside on Harrison's doorstep.

Looking at him, Alessandria realised that she could enjoy this moment of victory. For if she didn't try to enjoy the wins, then what was the point of them? There would always be more fights and people to stop, but true friends and family weren't in plentiful supply.

Turning her head back to the house, Alessandria smiled as she thought about Daniel and Harrison progressing in their relationship. They were in love, they cared about one another and Daniel had encouraged her to pursue a relationship. But should she?

Walking towards the dirt road, Alessandria and Nemesio didn't say a word to one another. Yet Alessandria knew he was smiling. Should she just ask? But what would she ask? She was Nobility and noblewomen don't ask out men. It's surely the other way around.

As the two heroes walked along the dirt road back to the castle, Alessandria felt the rough stones and sand under her leather boots, it finally dawned on her that this was her life. She might have been a Dominicus Procurator and a Noble Lady, but this was her life and she was determined to enjoy it. Especially, after almost losing everyone she loved today.

She gently grabbed Nemesio's wrist and asked: "It's still early evening, do you... want to get some dinner?"

Nemesio smiled.

"I thought you had paperwork to do?"

"It can wait. This can't,"

"Thank you. I would like dinner very much,"

AUTHOR'S NOTE

I really hope you enjoyed the book and this book, I definitely wanted to do quite a lot with it.

Originally, I was considering having the main plot of this book as a sort of legal setting with Alessandria having to prove a Noble person innocent of a crime. To win their House's support. But I decided against it. Maybe that will be a future idea.

Especially, since Alessandria needs to get the support of the other 4 Inquisitorial Orders, the House of Blueheart and the Church.

Anyway, in Heart of Lies, I really wanted to explore various relationships between the characters. For example, I wanted to see if Alessandria could find Nemesio attractive. Since I've tried to have romantic elements in my other books, but I always seem to end up killing them!

Thankfully, that didn't matter this time around.

Also, I wanted to see if Alessandria could

19

work through her feelings because we've all liked someone in the past and had to gather up the courage to ask someone out. So, I wanted to show Alessandria attempting to do that.

And before you ask no, I have no idea what happens on this date. Nor do I know if this date is going to have a short story dedicated to it. I might have to write the next book first to be able to figure that out.

Something else I wanted to explore in the book was Daniel after being tortured because of Nemesio. This I thought would be interesting to explore because I knew I would show his trauma. Yet I wanted to show his recovery too.

Now, because of my psychology background, I need to stress the chance of Daniel recovering from his psychological trauma within three weeks is near impossible. But I think the psychology part of myself can forgive me as I showed psychological therapy isn't an instant fix and it takes a while to complete. (Again, not shown in this book but it's fiction!)

The last relationship I wanted to explore was Daniel and Harrison. Mainly, because I wanted to explore the idea of sex in autistic relationships.

As a result, I can almost guarantee there are a few autistic people reading this book and I wanted to stress that if you're concerned about sex. It's okay and you aren't alone.

Overall, I really hope you enjoyed this book and I look forward to seeing you in another one!

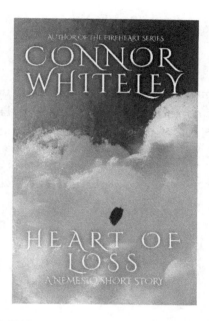

GET YOUR FREE AND EXCLUSIVE
SHORT STORY NOW! LEARN ABOUT
NEMESIO'S PAST!

https://www.subscribepage.com/fireheart

Thank you for reading.

I hoped you enjoyed it.

If you want a FREE book and keep up to date about new books and project. Then please sign up for my newsletter at www.connorwhiteley.net/

Have a great day.

About the author:

Connor Whiteley is the author of over 30 books in the sci-fi fantasy, nonfiction psychology and books for writer's genre and he is a Human Branding Speaker and Consultant.

He is a passionate Warhammer 40,000 reader, psychology student and author.

Who narrates his own audiobooks and he hosts The Psychology World Podcast.

All whilst studying Psychology at the University of Kent, England.

Also, he was a former Explorer Scout where he gave a speech to the Maltese President in August 2018 and he attended Prince Charles' 70th Birthday Party at Buckingham Palace in May 2018.

Plus, he is a self-confessed coffee lover!

OTHER SHORT STORIES BY CONNOR WHITELEY

Blade of The Emperor

Arbiter's Truth

The Bloodied Rose

Asmodia's Wrath

Other books by Connor Whiteley:

The Fireheart Fantasy Series

Heart of Fire

Heart of Lies

More Coming Soon!

The Garro Series- Fantasy/Sci-fi

GARRO: GALAXY'S END

GARRO: RISE OF THE ORDER

GARRO: END TIMES

GARRO: SHORT STORIES

GARRO: COLLECTION

GARRO: HERESY

GARRO: FAITHLESS

GARRO: DESTROYER OF WORLDS

GARRO: COLLECTIONS BOOK 4-6

GARRO: MISTRESS OF BLOOD

GARRO: BEACON OF HOPE

GARRO: END OF DAYS

Winter Series- Fantasy Trilogy Books

WINTER'S COMING

WINTER'S HUNT

WINTER'S REVENGE

WINTER'S DISSENSION

Miscellaneous:

THE ANGEL OF RETURN

THE ANGEL OF FREEDOM

CRIMES AGAINST PROPERTY

CRIMINAL PROFILING: A FORENSIC
PSYCHOLOGY GUIDE TO FBI
PROFILING AND GEOGRAPHICAL
AND STATISTICAL PROFILING.

CLINICAL PSYCHOLOGY

FORMULATION IN PSYCHOTHERAPY

Companion guides:

BIOLOGICAL PSYCHOLOGY 2ND
EDITION WORKBOOK

COGNITIVE PSYCHOLOGY 2ND
EDITION WORKBOOK

SOCIOCULTURAL PSYCHOLOGY 2ND
EDITION WORKBOOK

ABNORMAL PSYCHOLOGY 2ND
EDITION WORKBOOK

PSYCHOLOGY OF HUMAN
RELATIONSHIPS 2ND EDITION
WORKBOOK

HEALTH PSYCHOLOGY WORKBOOK

FORENSIC PSYCHOLOGY WORKBOOK

GET YOUR FREE BOOK AT:
WWW.CONNORWHITELEY.NET

CPSIA information can be obtained
at www.ICGtesting.com
Printed in the USA
LVHW020306160721
692872LV00007B/262

9 781914 081644